THE CENTUS
A LEGION OF PNEUMOS NOVELLA

H.B. RENEAU

VESALIAN PUBLISHING

ACKNOWLEDGMENTS

This book wouldn't have been possible without the help and input of family, friends, roommates, classmates, editors, and beta readers.

Special thanks go to my editor Lara Kennedy, and thank you also to Natalia Junqueira for her gorgeous cover design.

Finally, this book is dedicated to all those who fight for a cause greater than themselves, even when the way forward is far from clear.

"The true soldier fights not because he hates what's before them, but because he loves what's behind him."
    – G.K. Chesterton

Map of Loren
218 M.E.

the North
Port Tuálath
Port Cála
Port Galaén
Fertile Inlet
Eastern Plains
Port Mârfa
La
Southern Shield
Tibolé

In his nearly six years in the Bellatorio, Gaius Flavius had served under many incompetent commanders. But Millus Szerio had to be the worst. Most days Gaius could handle that. Most days he could consider the realities of bureaucratic incompetence with something akin to muted tolerance. Today was not one of those days.

Gaius heeled his horse on as he raced into the Bellatori camp, the frigid mountain wind cutting at his cheeks and sending his blood-red cloak flying behind him. Pulling up abruptly outside the Millus's tent, he swiftly dismounted, plucking off his plumed helm and bracing it under one arm as he stalked toward the tent flap. The two foot soldiers outside snapped to attention, thumping their chests in salute. Gaius returned the gesture, trying and failing to regulate his tone as he spat out a greeting.

"Centus Flavius, here to see Millus Szerio."

"Of course, Centus! The Millus is regrettably occupied at present. May we—"

"It is urgent," Gaius said, gray eyes narrowing to hooded slits. "I'll see him *now*."

Not waiting for them to open the flap, Gaius pushed past, throwing it open as he stalked inside. The tent room was warm, in stark contrast to the frigid temperatures outside. Gaius stopped short at the food-laden table, overflowing with the most scrumptious of delicacies. The soft tittering of laughter filled the warm interior. Millus Szerio had guests.

As his eyes adjusted to the shadowed interior, they flew from face to face, finally falling on the portly Millus Szerio. He reclined lazily on his side, gesturing with the thick turkey drumstick he held in one hand.

Gaius gritted his teeth, somehow managing to restrain the sneer he felt bubbling beneath the surface. He instead snapped to attention, loudly thumping the metal gauntlet of his forearm against his embossed leather cuirass with a clang that brought the entire dinner party up short, staring at him in surprise.

Szerio was the last to respond, only glancing up when he noticed his conversation partner to have been distracted from the no doubt enthralling tale he'd been sharing.

"Yes, Centus? Can't you see I'm otherwise occupied?"

"Sir!" Gaius responded, voice echoing. "I'm here with an urgent message from the front. My Bellators are poorly rationed, without the food or equipment we were promised. If we are to hold our position to the west—"

"Yes, yes, Centus, I received your communiques. The issue is being looked into."

Gaius felt his teeth ache as they ground together. He resisted the urge to stare pointedly at the lavishly decorated table overflowing with sweetmeats and pastries.

"Sir, the men and women who serve under me *need* to be properly rationed if we are to fulfill our mission. We cannot leave the western front—"

"Centus!" A note of annoyance crept into Szerio's voice as he leaned forward, drumming his fingers rhythmically against the chair arm. "I *told* you that the matter is being *looked into*. Now, please, you're disturbing my guests."

There was a soft tittering of laughter from the aforementioned dinner companions. A vein in Gaius's temple throbbed, and his hands curled into fists of their own accord. His rising rage was truly making it difficult to see straight. This man was not fit to wipe the scum from the boots of even the lowest foot soldier in the Bellatorio, who served admirably and with honor. Whereas this man, no doubt descended from ancient Marian nobility, had barely even seen a battlefield before being commissioned as a Millus and charged with the war's execution. Didn't he understand what was at *stake*? How could he sit here in his warm quarters, eating delicacies, while men and women starved on the battlefield? It was unconscionable.

"You are *dismissed*, Centus."

Gaius thought briefly about skewering Szerio then and there, taking his overpuffed ego down a few notches. Gaius's fingers twitched toward his sword's pommel, relishing the thought of unsheathing it and showing this man what a true Bellator looked like. Then he thought of his Bellators, huddling around barely concealed campfires, trying to keep warm and desperate for rations that only he could bring them. He realized with frustration that he'd have some difficulty doing that from inside a prison cell, which is undoubtedly where he'd end up if he treated this Millus as he deserved.

So instead, Gaius gave Szerio a curt nod before saluting and spinning on his heel as he stalked out of the room. He was met outside by Decius Braína. Her straw-colored hair was plaited in the Bellatori fashion, her icy blue eyes scanning the garrison. She raised one delicate eyebrow at him, and he realized with sudden embarrassment that he'd likely outpaced her some ways back. In the meantime, she'd caught up and wisely watered the horses after he'd dismounted in a rage.

"Any luck?" she asked, but seemed unsurprised when he shook his head, the success of his mission written on his face.

"Well, it was worth a try," she said. "We could try the quartermaster directly, see what the garrison itself can spare."

"It's no use," Gaius said, rubbing a hand across his face. "None of them will dare act without Szerio's direct say-so. Reallocating rations is an offense worthy of court martial."

She nodded. Decius Erin Braína had served under him for two years now. An uplander by birth, she'd grown up in a tiny fishing village near the Western Plains. Gaius didn't much care for uplanders, typically. He found them uneducated, provincial in their outlook, and hostile toward outsiders. But Braína was different, curious about the world and smart as a whip. She'd done well in the Bellatorio and was respected by both commanders and subordinates. She'd quickly risen through the ranks, one of the few female Bellators to have received a commission. Even two hundred years after women had been allowed to enlist, it was still an uncommon profession for them to pursue.

"Well, what is it you're plannin'?" she asked, offering him his horse's reins. At his shrug, she raised an eyebrow. "You know as well as I do that this isn't the end of it."

Gaius was about to reply when a young messenger boy appeared, standing awkwardly in the periphery. Gaius turned to eye the boy pointedly.

"A-are you Centus Flavius?" the boy sputtered. "I-I have a message for you, sir."

Gaius put his hand out for the message, intentionally ignoring Braína's knowing look. He certainly wasn't done fighting, but he refused to give her the satisfaction of having her suspicions confirmed. He flicked a coin to the boy in thanks, noting with satisfaction how the boy's face lit up. The messenger thanked him profusely before scampering away.

Unfurling the scroll, Gaius scanned its contents, brow furrowing further by the line.

"What is it?" Braína asked.

"It's a summons," he said, voice disbelieving even to his own ears. "A summons from Imperator Lanus. He wishes to see me."

Braína's eyebrows had shot up at the first mention of Imperator Lanus, chief commander of the entire Western Imperium.

"That's incredible," she said finally. "When?"

"Tomorrow. Apparently, he's making a brief stopover in camp tonight before continuing on his tour of the western front."

"Well, this is perfect. Ask him about the rations."

"Millus Szerio won't take kindly to that."

"Screw the old fatbag."

Gaius's head cocked toward her, eyebrows raised.

Her eyes narrowed. "He doesn't give a fig about any of us. You tried appealing to him directly. You brought your concerns, and he's done nothing. You are fully within your rights, no, your *responsibilities* as a commander, to take your request up the chain of command."

Gaius nodded, considering. The thought made him uneasy. He disliked complaining to a commander's boss about his behavior, preferring instead to settle his disputes in person. But Braína was right. He'd tried everything, and he wasn't about to return to his Bellators empty-handed. If Szerio wouldn't help him, then Gaius would have to go over his head.

CHAPTER

TWO

The next morning, Gaius found himself ushered into Imperator Lanus's quarters and left to wait alone for the commander's arrival. Gaius shifted his weight awkwardly, trying to resist the urge to stare at each item of furniture, even as his curiosity threatened to get the better of him. It was highly unusual for a summoned Centus to be asked to wait within the Imperator's own quarters. He'd expected to remain outside, summoned in only when the Imperator was ready to see him. So he just stood there, uncomfortable, not knowing whether to sit down or remain upright. He decided that standing was by far the safer option.

Imperator Lanus's quarters were Spartan in comparison with Millus Szerio's lavish accommodations. The tent held only a small cot, a miniature writing desk that could be folded up and easily transported, and a small writing chair. There was a trunk at the end of the cot, no doubt holding the Imperator's personal items. But it still surprised Gaius to see no other sign of the commander's person within the quarters. There were no drawn likenesses of family members or personal items of any sort. Even for a Bellatori commander in the field, this was austere.

Gaius snapped to attention at the sound of the Imperator's

6

approach. Lanus entered in a swirl of rapid conversation, two anxious aides in tow desperately jotting down the orders he spat out. Gaius remained at attention, waiting to be addressed, but the Imperator continued barking orders at the terrified aides. When he was through, he paused, looking from one to the other before a small smile tugged at the corners of his mouth.

"Cheer up there, lads, there's only a war on."

The two aides glanced between themselves, clearly unsure whether to laugh. Gaius felt a grin threatening to break through his own military decorum. It quickly vanished when the Imperator turned his hawklike amber eyes on Gaius himself. Gaius thumped forearm to chest briefly in salute.

"Imperator, sir! Centus Flavius, as requested."

"Yes, yes, Centus. Have a seat, please, join me. I was about to send for some lunch." Lanus waved a hand in silent dismissal of the two aides, who, with looks of relief, immediately fled.

Lunch? Gaius thought. It was barely midmorning.

"I eat lunch early," Lanus continued. "I break my fast at three and so am often famished by nine or ten."

Understandably, Gaius thought acerbically. But he couldn't help being impressed. He liked a man who rose early to get a jump on the day ahead. He nodded, taking a seat at the edge of a second folding chair, which Lanus pulled from beneath the cot.

"Apologies for the accommodations. I travel light, you see; far easier to make and ready camp as I tour the western front."

Gaius nodded. This made sense. From everything he'd heard about the Imperator, he was a well-known and widely loved commander, not least because he often took it upon himself to check in with even the lowest foot soldier. He made a point to ask not only about their mission but also their personal lives, often looking for ways he could be of service. He'd long been a personal hero of Braína's, Gaius knew.

"Flavius . . . Where have I heard that name before? I believe I may have served with a Flavius, back during the days of the Cross-Sea invasion. Any relation?"

Buoyed with pride, Gaius nodded, then cleared his throat as he shifted nervously.

"Yes, sir, my uncle Remus. He speaks highly of you."

"Indeed! Remus Flavius's nephew—that explains so much."

Gaius nodded again. His family had served in the Bellatorio for generations, had even been part of the campaign that had first brought the Marian Empire to Loren. The mantle had been passed from generation to generation over the years. While the firstborn had a duty to protect the family holdings and further the lineage, younger sons were expected to preserve the family honor through martial service. It had been a boon at the Academy Bellatori, where many of his professors had known or served with his uncle or great-uncle. The name Flavius had a reputation that had given him an edge when assigned a new command, no doubt contributing to him reaching the rank of Centus at a mere 25 years old. The Bellators beneath him had respected him, trusted the family's reputation for excellence. Though he knew it a privilege to bear the name, Gaius had often wrestled with the pressure that such assumptions brought.

"I've heard good things about you, Centus," Lanus said, jolting Gaius from his reminiscing. "Your subordinates respect you, and your commanders speak highly of you, although grudgingly, in some cases, if truth be told."

Szerio, no doubt, Gaius thought, mentally cursing the old buffoon yet again.

"It seems you have a penchant for making yourself heard on behalf of those in your command."

Gaius said nothing, unsure whether Lanus meant this as commendation or rebuke.

A smile tugged at the Imperator's lips. "I appreciate a leader who puts their Bellators first, before personal ambition. Your first duty is always to those who follow you, as is the duty of any leader. Too many lose sight of that."

Gaius was growing to like this Imperator by the minute. He was just about to open his mouth and ask about further rations for his Bellators, when Lanus continued, "I have need of a reliable Centus like yourself. There is a mission, one that I am not at liberty to speak openly about, but one that I believe someone with your particular skill set would excel at."

Gaius suppressed a smile but felt himself straighten slightly at the compliment. "Sir!"

"I understand your unit has had some supply issues, trouble acquiring the needed rations."

Gaius leaned forward, arms braced against his knees. "Yes, sir. I've brought this to the attention of Millus Szerio, but there have been some . . . *logistical issues* at play."

"Indeed," Lanus said, mouth set in a thin line. Gaius suspected that this was not the first complaint against Millus Szerio to have reached his desk. "I have heard of these *logistical issues*. Have no doubt that they are being addressed at the *highest* level possible."

Gaius felt the satisfying weight of vindication coil in his stomach at the thought of that pompous asshole getting the discharge he so rightfully deserved.

"But don't worry. I would not see you separated from your Bellators. This mission requires a centurium, such as yours, with the expertise and cohesion that your reputation suggests. So, assuming you take me up on my offer, I'll send for your Bellators immediately, and they'll meet you here. You'll travel back to the capital, where you'll receive further briefing on the specifics of your mission."

Gaius nodded, even as he chuckled inwardly at Lanus's use of the term "offer," knowing as well as anyone that there was no such thing as a volunteer in the Bellatorio, only "voluntold."

Still he paused, shifting slightly as he chose his words carefully. "Of course, sir, only, would that not—well, what reinforcements would be arriving to replace us?"

Lanus cocked his head at Gaius, eyeing him with amusement. "You think the fighting here on the western front is more important."

"Sir, I—"

"It's all right," Lanus continued, raising a hand to silence Gaius's protests. "I understand your concerns and find your sense of duty admirable." Lanus paused, giving Gaius a sidelong look. "How much do you know about your enemy here, Centus?"

Gaius stiffened, drawing himself to his highest seated height. "Of course! The Grumáerian tribes to the west have made various incursions through the mountain passes for centuries. Rather than face us directly in the south, they'd rather take the coward's route, slipping through mountain passes in the dead of winter, attacking at night so they have the element of surprise."

Gaius paused, eying the commander, who nodded absently. "Indeed. We've been fighting the Grumáerians ever since the Marian Empire's fall. We're the last bastion, Gaius, and they would see us destroyed. I'm sorry to say that they've taken their tactics *elsewhere.*"

Gaius's eyes widened, and he leaned forward slightly. "Elsewhere, sir?"

"The Southern Shield has always been a tricky problem. They're so different from us, Gaius, and even from the uplanders on the Lorenan mainland. They've always wanted independence. And with help from the Grumáerian insurgents . . . I'm afraid the situation is dire indeed. And I think you may be just the commander we need. But that's enough for now. You'll receive your full briefing when you return to Crîd Eálas."

Gaius nodded, already planning the message he'd send to his Bellators farther up the pass. He regretted leaving any job half-done, but it sounded like they really were needed elsewhere. From where he stood, some R&R back in the capital was just what they deserved—anything to get his Bellators out of the wretched winter here on the western front.

"Thank you, sir, I'm grateful for your trust. We'll make you proud."

The Imperator raised a hand. "Please, no gratitude necessary, only the due reward for loyal service to Loren. We are men of honor, and it is our duty to see the mission of the Bellatorio fulfilled in the best interests of Loren. That is all I care about, as I'm sure it is for you—and, of course, the well-being of those in your command."

Gaius nodded before jumping to his feet as the Imperator rose abruptly.

"It's settled, then. Take the rest of the day to prepare yourself for the journey. Your Bellators will be here by morning, and you leave immediately."

Gaius saluted again before striding from the tent at Lanus's dismissal. He was eager to find Braína and tell her the news. They were finally going to get the hell out of this forsaken place, and that was just about the best thing he'd heard all winter.

CHAPTER

THREE

As the men settled into camp after yet another day of hard riding along the winding western road to Crîd Eálas, Gaius occupied himself by seeing to his gear and reviewing the correspondence that had found its way to him via messenger, detailing the progress the rest of the Western Imperium was making against the raiders in the pass. Gaius had long ago discovered that the secret to life in the Bellatorio was to become accustomed to long stretches of monotony interjected with occasional excitement. Though he'd largely accepted this, he still couldn't bring himself to relish the prospect of another long day in the saddle.

Unfortunately, those in his command had found other sources of diversion. Gaius's head jerked up at the sounds of shouting, and he squinted against the evening sun to see two young Tiros working out their . . . *differences* in the open field at the center of camp.

"That, my friend, is a load of codswallop!" One of the young Bellators squinted his dark downlander eyes with suspicion.

His blond-haired companion glared back. "It's not! My grandda saw them with his own eyes!"

"He did nothing of the sort," the dark-haired one replied

haughtily, shaking his head as he made a face at the other Bellators nearby. This was met with loud guffaws as the blond's face reddened.

By this time, the ruckus had caught the attention of nearby ears. Gaius glanced backward at the pair, brows knitting together. The blond one's name was Diolun Maher, a young Tiro from the uplands somewhere to the north, Gaius remembered. Diolun was one of the few uplanders in the division, and his pale skin and blond hair—even cropped short in the Bellatori fashion—set him apart from the others.

"If I said that it happened, then it happened." Diolun's eyes glinted in anger as he glanced between laughing faces.

His dark-haired tormenter shook his head, snorting. "I'll believe that the ancient Lorenan savages built the first catapults the same day I meet the *faerie* king who leapt up from the hinterlands!"

His friends let out peals of laughter, and he grinned in triumph. "Just another silly uplander legend. Nothing more."

"That's not true." Diolun's hands balled into fists as the laughing grew louder.

Gaius glanced around in search of Sergius Tullius and spotted him lounging against a nearby tree, watching the ensuing argument play out. Gaius frowned. He understood allowing the men to work out their differences among themselves, especially the young, hotheaded Tiros, but this seemed to be getting a bit out of hand.

Gaius could intervene himself, of course, but he'd had it ingrained in him that these things were best handled at the lowest level of command possible. Involve himself too often, his superiors promised, and he'd soon find himself overwhelmed by the minutia of squabbles within the unit and quickly lose the broader perspective.

Still, Gaius thought it important that he understand something of the men and women who served under him. Moreover, there weren't many uplanders among Gaius's men, so Diolun stood out. As a people, they typically preferred to keep to themselves and distrusted the Bellatorio on principle. Diolun shared this dislike for authority, if his starring role in Decius Braína's not-infrequent reports of disorderly conduct among the men were to be believed. Gaius's second-in-command had told him as much, often singling Diolun out as a Bellator in need of rebuke or repercussions for some incursion.

Yet Gaius suspected she had a soft spot for the young Bellator that shared her heritage, if only discernible by the particular care she took to put him in his place when he got into trouble.

As if summoned by his thoughts, Braína appeared, stalking across the camp yard toward the pair of Tiros just squaring up for a fight. Gaius watched with growing concern as the group of downlanders began circling young Diolun, whose glare and shouted epithets suggested he wasn't about to back down.

Gaius sighed, glancing at the still-reclined Sergius Tullius, who was chuckling at the fight about to break out in front of him. With a shout, Diolun lunged at Marcus, socking him in the nose before his friends could react. Shaking his head, Gaius heaved himself to his feet and began striding toward them. Braína reached them first and, dodging a wayward swing, wrestled the two Tiros apart with the help of one of Marcus's friends.

"What in Pneumos's name is goin' on 'ere?" Braína growled, holding each young man by the ear like impudent schoolboys. Diolun and Marcus had stopped resisting, but they still eyed each other warily. Blood dripped slowly from Marcus's nose. Neither said anything.

"No answers? Oh, wonderful, I suppose I get to guess, then. Unfortunately for you, I neither know nor care what could possibly possess two commissioned Bellators in the Lorenan military to reduce themselves to petty schoolboy squabbles."

Seeing that she had things well enough in hand, Gaius paused, not wanting to intervene unless he was needed. By this time, Sergius Tullius had belatedly heaved himself to his feet and ambled toward them. Seeing his approach, Braína turned her glare on him.

"Sergius Tullius," she said sharply. "It would seem that men under your command were engagin' in disorderly conduct. Were you plannin' on intervenin'?"

Tullius's eyes narrowed, but he gave a curt nod. With a wan smile, he replied, "No harm done, Decius. It's good for the lads to have it out every once in a while, 'specially the uplanders. Hotheads to a man, you see. I understand your womanly distaste for violence, though, and will be sure to keep a tighter rein in future."

Gaius saw Braína and Diolun both stiffen and felt like rubbing his eyes. *Oh boy*, he thought.

Braína dropped the ears of the two Tiros and turned her whole frame toward the Sergius, arms crossed as she gave him a withering glare. Though he was a whole head taller than her, Gaius thought he saw Tullius deflate slightly under that piercing gaze, but only slightly.

"I think there may have been some misunderstandin', Sergius," Braína said, voice icy. The surrounding Tiros shifted uneasily as they glanced at each other, unsure what to do when their superiors began bickering among themselves.

"And what is that?" Tullius asked.

"As to your job description," Braína continued. "You see, as your *superior*, I must remind you that your job is to maintain order and discipline amongst the men. I don't care if you think they need to 'have it out.' That's what extra duty is for. And as for my *womanly* distaste, I assure you, it is purely focused on the incompetence I have witnessed today. Any of that unclear, Sergius?"

Tullius's eyes narrowed, and he moved an inch closer. To her credit, Braína stood her ground until she was glaring up into Tullius's beady eyes. Tullius opened his mouth as if to say something, at which point Gaius reached them.

"Do we have a problem here, Decius?" he asked.

At his approach, the Tiros all snapped to attention. Braína and

Tullius were slower, letting their glares settle a moment longer before turning to salute him.

"None, Centus," Braína replied. "Merely sortin' out a dispute among the men. The two Tiros here will be pullin' extra kitchen duty for the next month."

Gaius nodded, leveling a stern gaze at the two boys, who looked appropriately abashed. "Indeed. That sounds appropriate. Clearly, their current duties leave them insufficiently occupied. Now, I'm afraid I need your assistance, Decius. If you would be so kind?" Gaius motioned for her to follow him, and with a parting glare at the sullen-looking Tullius, she complied.

WHEN THEY REACHED HIS TENT, Gaius gestured toward a chair, urging Braína to take a seat.

"You didn't have to do that, sir," she murmured petulantly. "I had things well in hand."

Gaius snorted. "*Did* you now? From where I was standing, it looked like you were about two wrong words away from an altercation with our most senior Sergius."

At first, Braína said nothing and Gaius glanced at her, seeing her eyes narrow.

"The man's a bigoted pig, *sir*. He wants uplanders like Diolun Maher in the Bellatorio about as much as he wants women. He'd be more than happy to see both of us bullied out before he'd lift a finger."

Gaius sighed, rubbing his eyes roughly. "He's from another generation, Braína. Things were diff—"

"It doesn't matter." Braína's voice was flat. "With all due respect, sir, it simply doesn't matter."

Gaius gritted his teeth, considering. "You're right, Braína. It *shouldn't* matter. But Tullius has been in the Bellatorio longer than either one of us has been alive. He knows his way inside and out of a combat situation, and, well, we need him."

Braína's lips pressed thinly together before she nodded. "Yes, sir."

"Cheer up, Decius," Gaius said. "You'll prove yourself soon enough."

Braína cocked her head at him, eyes serious but with a slight dimpling in one cheek.

"Understood, sir. But with all due respect, I shouldn't have to."

CHAPTER

FOUR

To Gaius's mind, it seemed the closer they got to the capital, the rowdier and bawdier the songs of his Bellators became.

Ohhhhh I went down to Crîd Eálas,
Pride of Bellatori prowess
Met a wynnie, lithe and rangy
Pretty, cheery, and gettin' frisky.
Life's a laugh and death's a joke
But the pixies want that crimson cloak!

Gaius smiled slightly at the familiar marching tune. He knew it well but declined to participate. As the commander, he had to maintain some sense of decorum. It was all well and good for the Centus to have a sense of humor, but not at the expense of order and discipline. Decius Braína, on the other hand, held no such compunction.

"That's not the way I heard it," she exclaimed. "From all accounts, *you* were the one offering the extra coin for a few more minutes, Gallagn! Couldna quite make it 'appen, there, could you?"

The line of soldiers guffawed, and Gaius shook his head. Braína

18

grinned triumphantly and elbowed him in the side.

"Go on, then. You know it was funny."

Gaius snorted, shaking his head, and ignored the smirk she shot him.

As they rounded the last hill overlooking Crîd Eálas, Gaius couldn't help the small flip-flop of his stomach as he spied the tall, white, shining walls of the city, the mighty Vindolum rising above it all. Braína must have seen something in his face, because she suddenly clapped him on the back.

"And who, might I ask, are you thinking about, Centus?" She raised an eyebrow in a knowing look.

Gaius cleared his throat. "Nothing, Decius. Only the provisions that must be made for the journey."

"Oh, really?" she replied. "Not at all of one particular businesswoman?"

Gaius busied himself searching through his saddlebag.

Braína laughed. "I'm sure she'll be happy to see you as well, sir."

He glanced at her and saw something flash in her eyes. His brow furrowed, but it was gone as quickly as it had come. She turned back to the Bellators that marched behind them.

"Almost there, now, boys," she called. "We'll have you back in time for full bellies and warm beds!"

"Hopefully, someone else to warm them!" one of the young Tiros called in response. The Bellators laughed in agreement, Braína included, as she turned back to continue next to Gaius down the western road to Crîd Eálas.

THAT AFTERNOON, Gaius left his men to their ale and companions in the main tavern, taking the stairs two at a time to the floor above. Brushing off probing fingers and smiling eyes with an apologetic smile, he made his way toward the top floor, where he knew he would find her.

A quick knock at the only door on the top landing, and the murmured reply was as much invitation as he needed. He pushed open the door, and there she was.

Figure framed against the light streaming in from the round window overlooking the city, shutters thrown open to the cool spring breeze, Aelianna Manius stood as a woman transfixed, overlooking her own little kingdom amid the sprawl of the capital. She turned slightly, long, thickly coiled curls swishing against her golden, honey-colored back as she turned one soft, dark eye toward him. One arched eyebrow was raised in question as the heart-shaped curve of her mouth smiled in knowing welcome.

He'd crossed the room in two steps and had his arms around her by the third. He felt her melt against him, and he wanted nothing more than to pull her closer. His lips found hers, and he felt something inside himself give way, unfolding and releasing a stress he hadn't even known he carried. He lifted a hand to her chin even as the other gripped tighter her waist. He felt her head tilt back, mouth opening slightly toward him, and the briefest flicker of tongue against his lips.

He wanted her intensely in that moment, and it took every ounce of willpower for him not to take her right then. Instead, he pulled his face back an inch, still breathing in the intoxicating aroma of her skin.

"Well, hello to you too," she murmured, breath tickling the skin of his neck and making gooseflesh ripple across his arms. He cleared his throat, trying to regain some composure and failing miserably.

"It's, uh, good to see you, Aelianna. I've—well, it's been too long."

She chuckled. "Cold nights on the western front, I take it?"

He felt her brush her lips against the hollow at the base of his throat, and he swallowed. "Frigid."

She smiled and turned away, grabbing his hand as she did so and leading him toward the lounge chair in the far corner of the room. She pulled him down to the chair as she began systematically untying each piece of his armor with practiced fingers, as only a woman of her trade could. "Tell me."

He did, unburdening himself of every pain and frustration of the past few months, letting them fall away from him as surely as the pieces of his armor slid to the floor. He told her about the incompetence of commanders like Szerio and the miseries of winter on the western front. He told her funny stories of pranks pulled by his men, exaggerated tales of valor that they'd spun wide over campfires, and even the excitement of Imperator Lanus's offer.

Aelianna was duly impressed. She knew how hard he'd worked to live up to his family name, knew what this recognition meant for him. Still, a small frown creased her brow as she cocked her head at him, considering.

"So, the Southern Shield, then? That's where you're heading?"

Gaius nodded, taking one of her hands from where they'd folded after their task was done. He cradled it in one of his own as he traced the creases of her palm with a finger. "Yes, I can't say for how long." His eyes met hers, and he saw her frown deepen. "What is it?"

"Well, it's just that we aren't at war with them, are we? As one of Loren's own provinces, it seems odd that there should be armed forces there."

Gaius shook his head, suddenly realizing he probably ought to have been a little less specific with their exact destination. Still, it was Aelianna. He'd known her for years and knew she'd say nothing to jeopardize their mission.

"Then why?" she asked. "Why send in Bellators?"

Gaius shrugged. "There are insurrectionists making trouble on the larger islands. They need us to come take care of it."

Aelianna's lips pursed into a thin line as her eyes narrowed slightly. "That hardly seems the job of the Bellatorio."

Gaius chuckled, pulling her toward him. "I know, yet another thing to take me away from you. But it also brought me here now, so in many ways, it's a blessing, isn't it?"

He bent his head toward her, kissing slowly up the length of her jaw, closing his eyes as he inhaled the floral scent of her hair. She pulled abruptly away. He stared at her, surprised to see her jaw clench and her eyes tighten.

"Believe it or not, your company is not always first on my thoughts."

Stung, Gaius could only blink at her, aghast at what to say to that. She must have seen his hurt expression, because her face quickly softened. "I only mean that, as a concerned citizen, I wonder what precedent it sets that the Bellatorio is the first force sent in to quell all domestic matters."

Gaius chuckled awkwardly. Aelianna had always had unconventional political opinions, but even he wasn't exactly sure what to make of this. Yet he was equally perturbed by the extra six inches that now lay between them. He settled on the diplomatic route.

"Aelianna, you know as well as I do that the Bellatorio is charged with keeping the peace in all regions of Loren."

She rolled her eyes, fixing him with a knowing look. "Yes, but I also know that the Southern Shield is Lorenan in name only. Their culture is entirely different. Surely in this case, some sort of home policing would be—"

Gaius couldn't help the snort that escaped his throat, though he instantly regretted it upon receiving Aelianna's withering look in return. Quickly sobering, he sought for a reasoning tone. "Surely you can't expect the Regio to stand idly by while a region within his domain seeks open secession?"

Aelianna's chin jutted out in that adorable way she had. "Why not?"

Gaius opened and closed his mouth, gaping at her. Did she really not understand why that was so ludicrous?

Taking advantage of his pause, she continued, "The Southern Shield were free states prior to the Marian invasion. I don't see why—"

"Because it completely undermines our standing in the

region!" He knew that a note of condescension had crept into his voice, but he couldn't help it. He was aghast at her naivete. "How would it look to our allies and enemies alike if we allowed one of our own provinces to simply leave, especially a strategically valuable one that protects our southern coast from invasion?"

Aelianna's eyes flashed for a moment before settling on an ice-cold detachment. "Well, of course you would have to say that, wouldn't you?"

"What's that supposed to mean?"

Aelianna sighed, pinching the bridge of her nose with one hand, before looking up at him. "Only that you're allowed to form your own opinions, you know. You're not your family, and you're certainly not the Bellatorio." Her voice had softened as she spoke, and she stared up at him with a look of concern before slipping her fingers deftly into his.

Gaius felt himself deflate, his anger vanishing as quickly as it had flared. There was something about Aelianna. He never could stay angry with her. He squeezed her fingers before replying, "But I am, Aelianna. You know that." His voice held a note of resignation, yet it was tinged with pride. This was the life he had chosen, even if it had been laid out for him. She looked like she was about to argue but then shook her head. On an impulse, he grabbed her other hand and pulled them both toward him.

"Marry me, Aelianna."

She snorted, shaking her head. "Not this again, Gaius. You know I can't do that."

Not giving up that easily, he persisted, drawing her chin up with one hand so that her eyes met his gaze. "Why not?"

She sighed. "We've been here before, Gaius," she said, slipping a hand out of his grip to rub wearily at her eyes. "I would be a terrible Bellatori wife. You know that."

Gaius shook his head. They *had* had this conversation before, but he remained undeterred. "I don't care."

"Maybe not now, Gaius. But you have your entire career ahead of you. You know better than anyone how political the Bellatorio is. If you marry me, then you'll never make Millus. How would it look? Having a whore for a Millus's wife."

He flinched at the word and was about to protest, but she continued, a note of pride swelling in her voice.

"Besides, I'm happy with my life, Gaius. I'm a businesswoman. I built this place from the ground up. If I married you, I couldn't be happy, not with you gone most of the year and me surrounded by the simpering lot of wives your comrades keep."

Gaius did protest at that. "You barely know them. How can you judge them so harshly?"

Aelianna cocked her head at him, giving him a long, sharp look. "I judge them because they would judge me, Gaius. You know they would." She shook her head. "I have no place in that world, and no desire to join it."

Gaius was quiet, mulling over her words. He knew she had a point but was unwilling to give up quite that easily. Perhaps it was a battle for another day, though. As if reading his thoughts, Aelianna moved in closer and pinched his chin between thumb and forefinger, drawing it down so he was looking directly at her.

"Listen to me, Gaius Flavius," she said firmly, without warmth or humor. "I do not need *saving*. I do not need you to rescue me and whisk me away from this life. I *chose* this path. It may not be for everyone, but it is most certainly mine. And I will thank you to respect my choice in the matter."

At the look in her eye, he could do nothing but nod. Her expression softened, and her grip turned smoother, almost caressing, as her fingers trailed down his throat and curled around the back of his neck. She drew his face toward her as she reached up to him. His breath caught as her warm lips trailed along his jaw, and he gasped as she caught the lobe of one ear between her teeth. Playfully, she tugged at it, and his body reacted viscerally. He ached to touch her, but something held him back. He hesitated, and she released him, breath tickling his ear as she whispered, "But tonight, Gaius Flavius, I choose you."

And with that, she pulled him down to her.

CHAPTER

FIVE

It was the rainy season when they'd arrived in the Southern Shield, and Gaius couldn't remember the last time he'd been so thoroughly soaked. He'd known to expect foul weather, heard stories of the monsoons that struck the tiny island shores at the simplest provocation and horror stories of the sea storms that would come out of nowhere, wrecking hapless ships against its rocky shores. He'd known in the way one knows things intellectually, but nothing could have prepared him for the visceral shock of the damp, cold tendrils that curled up his spine, the incessant moisture that crept into every item of clothing and bedding.

As he sat huddled under an oilskin, shivering as the dew crept into every piece of fabric he wore, he decided that this was a whole new level of misery. It wasn't enough that the Southern Shield was cursed with all manner of insects, whether flying, crawling, or in any other manner creeping, but they also had to infiltrate every nook and cranny of the village. Yet, even worse than the physical miseries was the agony of waiting.

They'd arrived nearly a month before, eager and ready to meet their mission's objectives and expecting to make enemy contact almost immediately. The briefing they'd received in the capital had described a vigilante group that had wrested control of the main island of Tibolé, where they were to land. It had been not-so-subtly implied that they should expect the enemy to find *them* before *they* found the enemy. As a result, they'd hastened in their preparations and fortifications, expecting at any moment to be overrun by savage adversaries.

And yet the days continued to creep by, one steamy, water-logged day bleeding into the next. Gradually, the cohort lost that sense of buoyant excitement with which they had arrived. They'd hoped to complete this new mission quickly and receive the glory and recognition they'd been promised. With every passing day, the likelihood of a prolonged stay loomed larger.

In truth, the days and nights of endless rain and the daily treks would have been enough to quickly sour the mood. What's more, Gaius had heard nothing of the promised show of force that would provide them with backup once they made contact. In the daily messages he sent to Imperator Lanus, he repeatedly asked when such a force would arrive. Yet his messages were each met with silence. They'd received no further communication or instructions since their arrival, and their fortifications lay as yet untested. Meanwhile, morale continued to crumble as the Bellators grew tired of meager rations and miserable living conditions. He'd had to personally break up at least two minor brawls among the Tiros, unsurprised to find the uplander Diolun Maher smack in the middle of both.

Gaius slapped a mosquito that landed on the back of his neck, missing it by mere millimeters. The sound was loud enough to startle the arriving messenger boy, who jumped back in alarm, the letter he held crumpled in one hand.

"Sir?" The boy's eyes were wide with fear as Gaius glanced at him.

"What?"

The boy shot him a look that clearly stated he was unsure whether to stay or flee. Gaius sighed. "Yes, yes. What is it?"

Summoning his courage, the boy continued, "You've received a message, sir!"

Gaius sat up eagerly, arm outstretched. "Well, go on then!"

The boy quickly placed the message in Gaius's hand before scampering off back to the mess tent.

Gaius quickly cracked the seal, recognizing Imperator Lanus's insignia. He scanned the page, excitement coursing through him.

Finally, he thought.

The message gave detailed instructions for the exact time and place that Gaius's men were to engage the enemy. According to the Imperator's informants, the enemy force had similarly barricaded themselves. It would therefore require an all-out assault to break them from their fortifications.

As Gaius and Erin Braína made their way through the small marketplace in the coastal village nearest the enemy encampment, Gaius couldn't help but think that much of life on the island of Tibolé was not as it seemed to be. The largest island of the archipelago that made up the Southern Shield, Tibolé was home to a people of quiet yet hardy stock. Distrustful of outsiders, they kept to themselves, and they had met the Bellatori unit in their midst with suspicion and disdain.

The message from Imperator Lanus had told little, save the structure of the encampment. It had given no numbers, either of combatants or any civilians that might be nearby. It said only of its purpose that the encampment was there to guard the activities of the insurrectionists, who operated a smuggling ring out of this port. Gaius didn't know much about the Southern Shield. But he knew that it was an important site of resources, include a valuable metal called Tellurium. And there was a thriving fur trade of large rodents that the locals called Dínue.

If he hadn't known better, he would have assumed this port and the thriving village that surrounded it to be perfectly harmless. But upon further scouting of the area, the encampment of armed men nearby had proved sufficiently damning. This brought them to their current task, scouring the village for any information they could glean from its inhabitants.

"Remind me why we're 'ere again?" Braína muttered, shooting a defiant look at a group of men who'd stopped their conversation midsentence to glare at them. The nearest one bent to spit on the ground near their feet as the two of them passed.

"Let it go," Gaius murmured, placing a restraining hand on Braína's arm as he felt her stiffen beside him. "It's not worth it. Besides, we've got a job to do."

"Waste of time is more like it," Braína growled. "This lot ain't gonna tell us nothin'."

Gaius grimaced, but he couldn't help thinking she was likely correct. Culturally distinct from the mainland Lorenans, the islanders of the Southern Shield had come to fall under the Regio's rule purely by proximity and the practical necessities that the Marian Empire had for governing its various provinces. In language, religion, culture, and creed, the natives of the Southern Shield, or as they called themselves, the Udánma, could not have been more different from their fellow mainland Lorenans. During their brief stop in the capital, Gaius had tried to find out what information he could, knowing it would be valuable in the coming campaign. But information was limited, even in the capital's largest libraries. Few had taken the time to understand the native culture of the islands. And what records he could find were written solely by outsiders. No firsthand accounts existed, as far as he could find.

Gaius was about to admit defeat and tell Braína that they should head back to camp, when an older woman at the far end of the market square caught his eye. The woman was clothed in the traditional dress of the islands, the bark cloth of her skirt decorated in ornate geometric designs that made Gaius go cross-eyed if he stared too long at them. He watched as her fingers moved quickly over a felted piece of bark cloth, an ink-dipped reed brush carving steep lines and curves into the textured surface. On impulse, Gaius moved toward her, stopping to admire her work as the images came into focus.

Unlike the usual geometric designs of the islands, this piece of bark cloth was decorated with images of people, figures dancing in a line across the length of the fabric.

"Y'know the story, eh?"

Startled from his close inspection of the drawing, Gaius glanced up to see the woman regarding him closely. Her skin was the color of burnt sienna, and lines creased at the corners of warm amber eyes that seemed to look right through him. Gaius swallowed, his throat suddenly dry, and shook his head. The woman inclined her head, clearly suspecting as much, and bent to resume her work. Looking closer, Gaius could see that the pictures moved in a progression across the length of the fabric.

"It is the story of the Le'ena, the spirit-binders who serve the great Cála, who brought the island up from the ocean floor. Le'ena protect the islands from the churning waves seeking always to devour them, a place set apart from the chaos of the world."

Gaius could see two figures dancing across the fabric, scenes of love intertwined with scenes of violence as the two fought off shadow creatures that emerged from the waves. The central image of the fabric showed the two figures standing arm in arm. One reached upward, a swirling substance pouring from its hand and forking out into the many-limbed branches of a massive tree, while the other pointed downward, forming the tree's intricate root system. The whole composition seemed almost to move in a swirling, inky mass as Gaius's eyes lost focus. He blinked, and the effect disappeared. He looked up then to meet the woman's knowing eyes. He opened his mouth to ask more about these "spirit- binders," when the sound of approaching feet stopped him.

"These grelún be bother you, eh, marné?" The group of men from before had sidled up to listen to their conversation. By then, Braína had also joined him, and Gaius felt her stiffen as her hand moved toward the hilt of her sword. He shot her a warning look before turning to the men. He opened his mouth to explain that their inquiries were entirely harmless, when the older woman's voice cracked sharply.

"Ah, you lot be stirrin' trouble, eh? You best be goin' home. No need for dat here!"

To Gaius's surprise, the group of men looked frankly abashed, and with one sidelong glance back at Gaius and Braína, the men sidled away, presumably back to their homes.

"Thank you," Braína said, turning back to the older woman. "We don't want trouble, to be sure."

The woman eyed her with one raised brow. "True-true? Why then you be 'ere? You with your swords and your arrows? Why you 'ere if no be trouble?"

Gaius stepped toward her, voice low and beseeching. "We're here to prevent trouble, madam. The Bellatorio has received word that insurrectionists are planning a revolt on the islands. Have you heard word of any such activities in these parts?"

The woman snorted, pivoting back to continue painting the geometric designs on the felted bark cloth before her. "I know of none of that 'ere."

Gaius knelt beside her then, fixing her with the steeliest gaze he could muster. "Madame, if we don't stop this uprising before it starts, then I'm afraid there will be violence. If you know anything at all, I must strongly urge you to come forward."

The woman matched his gaze look for look, and Gaius was startled by the intensity behind those dark amber eyes. "Boy, you listen 'ere. There forever be those who make trouble, de young ones who have nothing to lose—lives new and ready to be wasted. Boys, just like you," she added, brandishing her paintbrush toward him. "But I tell you true-true, the king across the water who you serve, he has nothing to fear from Udánma. We want only live 'ere on our island, the way we 'ave for centuries. You 'ere? You bring nothing but chaos wit' you."

Gaius's lips pressed into a thin line as the woman turned resolutely back to her work, the conversation clearly over. He glanced at Braína, who gave him a shrug and an "I told you so" sort of smirk. Reluctantly, he rose from his kneeling position, and the two of them made their way out of camp.

"She's lying," Gaius said on the road back to the encampment. "There's no possibility that there's an encampment of insurrectionists not an hour's walk from the village and nobody knows a thing about it." Frustration crept into his voice, making his words sharper than intended.

Braína only shrugged. "You said yourself, the islanders have no loyalty to Loren and no love for the Bellatorio. Is it really surprisin' that they'd be a bit close-lipped?"

Gaius nodded, unable to fault her reasoning. But something about the encounter still made him hesitate. There was an air about the older woman, a directness that spoke of someone with enough authority to have no need for guile or misdirection. *She may be highly respected among her people*, he reminded himself. *But I'm an outsider, a "grelún." There's no reason to think she'd be truthful with me.* Reassured by his own reasoning, Gaius pushed the niggling feeling of doubt to the back of his mind. There'd be time for that sort of questioning later. For now, he had an assault to plan.

CHAPTER
SIX

As the night darkened and shadows stretched low, Gaius gazed through the reeds at the flickering fires of the small encampment. He thought he could hear music and laughter filling the night air. The drumbeats and lutes of traditional island music permeated the warm stillness of the night. The advanced force of his centurium had staked out their position around midday and then waited silently for darkness to fall. He'd left a reserve regiment back at the garrison, and another on the beaches where he'd received word that the reinforcements should be landing. With the intelligence he'd been given, he should have more than enough men to take this encampment. He hadn't expected this, though. This sounded like some sort of celebration, and Gaius worried that it meant more civilians were likely to be in the area. His thoughts flashed to the woman in the village with those knowing amber eyes, and he shook his head.

It didn't matter now. After all, they had a job to do. The message he'd received from Imperator Lanus had been clear about what their mission was in the Southern Shield. They'd obtained ideal positioning and would launch the assault as soon as the outpost of armed men had settled in for the night. If all went according to plan, the enemy would be caught wholly unaware. Gaius glanced up at the rising moon. Luckily, he saw only a faint sliver, yielding barely enough light. It would hide their movements well. Looking around, he spied Decius Braína, her pale blue eyes watching and waiting for the signal she knew would come. He gave her a curt nod, and she gestured to the Bellators around her, urging them to ready for the coming assault.

Gaius crept toward the encampment, keeping low to the ground. The high grass of the marshlands tickled his legs as he moved through the blackness. He could feel the shuffle of feet behind him, the presence of men on both sides, but could barely see beyond his own outstretched arms. Raising his hand in signal, he motioned for them to spread out, surrounding the encampment. There'd be no insurgents escaping on his watch. Their intelligence suggested the encampment held only twenty or so men, poorly equipped, as so many in the Southern Shield were. These were rebels only, insurrectionists and smugglers set on undermining the Marian crown's hold on the islands. They were no match for the discipline of Bellatori steel.

The smell of cooking fires was the first to greet his senses, long before he heard the murmur of whispered conversation and glimpsed the flicker of flames. He signaled to the others to drop lower beneath the tall, shielding tendrils of the jungle grass they waded through. The enemy had left sentries out, their shadows just visible as they patrolled beyond the spiked barricades.

It was to be expected, he decided. Even rabble knew better than to leave their position undefended. As they grew closer to the barricade, Gaius felt a nervous twinge grip his stomach at the sight of at least a dozen sentries.

Did they suspect an attack? Why have so many of their men on guard?

Gaius glanced backward, just making out the nervous excitement on the faces of the five young Tiros in his cohort, including the troublemakers Diolun and Marcus. Not trusting them to their own devices, Gaius had specifically assigned them to his own personal unit. It was only now, with the uncertainty of what lay ahead, that he wondered if that had been such a good idea after all.

He glanced back at the encampment, swiftly recounting in his mind. Yes, definitely twenty sentries. Had their scouts been wrong? Or had the insurrectionists grown in number since the last intelligence report? He had to assume that there were more men asleep in the tents that dotted the encampment. Sure, they had the advantage of surprise, but they'd certainly be outnumbered nonetheless.

Should I risk it?

The memory of Imperator Lanus's words echoed in his mind. *We serve at the pleasure of Loren and the Marian crown. Can I trust you to do your duty, Gaius?*

And that was that.

Gritting his teeth, Gaius froze, one hand raised to the men behind, who waited with bated breath for the signal they knew would come. Gaius paused, watching as the nearest sentry moved precisely between the opening of two spiked barricades, and he let his hand fall.

An earsplitting horn echoed into the night, and Gaius lunged for the sentry. His gaze met the man's widened eyes as he turned and spotted Gaius's hulking form springing from the darkness. With a savage slice of his sword, Gaius raked the blade across the man's exposed neck, watching as blood spurted, splattering the jungle ground with drops of red. The man's eyes widened further, and a wet gurgling sound emanated from his throat before he collapsed to his knees. He clutched futilely at his collar before crumpling into a heap as he lay still beneath the growing shadow of an oozing pool.

Gaius paused for a moment but shrugged off the sight like an old, worn traveling cloak, adroitly shedding the inessential and encumbering emotions that accompanied the act. From elsewhere in the encampment, he could hear the shouts and clangs of metal that signified imminent combat. Braína and her forces would make their assault from the south. The time was now.

Spinning around, he saw that the young Tiros who followed him had made quick work of the other two sentries in this sector and were watching him expectantly, waiting for further instructions.

Gaius gestured for them to follow him as they made their way toward the central tent. Their scouts may have been wrong about the encampment's numbers, but their task was clear. They were to confiscate the smugglers' records and coin in the name of the Marian crown, anything that might prove the insurrectionist intent of these rebels.

There was a flurry of movement to his right, and Gaius spun to meet the blade of a behemoth of a man, bedecked in nothing but cropped trousers but screaming as he brandished a torch and a club the width of Gaius's leg.

"Back-a-ya, Marian scum!" the man shrieked, sweeping his staff in an arc that passed mere inches from Gaius's head. Gaius jerked backward, raising his blade and angling toward the giant.

"Yield, sir!" Gaius yelled, though his words were whisked away from him, unheard in the cacophony of shouts and screams from the encampment's inhabitants, all suddenly very much aware of the encroaching presence.

The man continued to advance, swinging his long club and forcing back the Tiros that had rushed to Gaius's aid.

"Yield in the name of Loren and the Marian crown," Gaius tried again, slowly circling in search of the giant's blind side.

"I do'na see no such crown," the man growled. With a sickening crack, his club made contact with one young Tiro's knee, extending it backward in a grotesque shape. The young man shrieked as he collapsed to the ground. Gaius lunged forward just as the giant's club swung toward the writhing Tiro. Gaius's sword sliced upward through the man's beefy chest and between his ribs. The man choked up a torrent of blood and sagged against Gaius, who, dislodging his sword, rolled him to the ground, where he collapsed in a heap.

Signaling for the Tiro Diolun to help him, he dragged the

moaning Bellator out of the main thruway. *What was his name? Cassius? Cato?* Gaius forced the boy's face up to look at him, noted his brow glazed with sweat, and pushed a sword into the young Tiro's clammy fist.

"Wait here, lad. We'll be back for you, but just now I can't spare the men to take you back to camp."

The boy nodded, fear tightening his eyes but jaw clenched in determination. Gaius patted his shoulder, feeling a churning in his own stomach at the look of absolute faith and trust the boy gave him. In that moment, he felt utterly unworthy of it.

Pushing the thought away, he gestured for the others to follow him. Rounding around the nearest tent, they made straight for the headquarters they'd been told lay at the center of the encampment. *Come on*, Gaius thought. *Let at least one thing go right tonight.* His eyes danced across the flickering shadows of men on tent walls, ignoring the shouts and clangs of steel that echoed around the encampment. *Where are you?*

Rounding the last row of tents, Gaius spotted it, the only stone building of the entire encampment, exactly in the center, where it'd been described.

Gaius froze.

Eyes widening, he watched as insurrectionists poured from that very building, heading straight for them. With a swell of fear, Gaius signaled for his Tiros to form up in a half circle to meet the onslaught. Diolun and Marcus immediately flanked him on either side, and Gaius felt the tension in both boys' stances.

"Easy," he murmured. "Let them come. We're well-armed and well-trained. They know that as well as anyone."

The boys nodded, but Gaius heard the note of fear in his own voice. He was right; they were better prepared. But they were also outnumbered five to one.

"Sound the horn," Gaius murmured. His eyes darted from one man to the next, searching desperately for any way out of this mess. But the ring of insurrectionists just continued to grow thicker. He swung his sword around, daring them to step closer, within range of its arcing bite.

They paused, eyeing him, and a few shouted epithets their way.

"What do we do, sir?" Marcus murmured to his left.

"Blow the horn again," Gaius said. Dutifully, the Tiro behind him let out its piercing wail.

Nothing.

This was not supposed to happen, Gaius thought. There were supposed to be twenty or thirty rebels at the most. In reality, there must have been close to one hundred. How could their intelligence have been so *wrong*?

My men are going to die.

These men, who had volunteered to fight for him, who had followed him into this mess, their lives would be forfeit because he had failed them. The misery that accompanied this realization bore down on him, far heavier than any fear he may have felt for his own sake.

I've failed them.

Out of the darkness, an earsplitting howl cut through the night as Decius Braína emerged, sword in hand, cutting through the mass of insurrectionists, her unit of Tiros falling in close behind. Not about to miss this opportunity, Gaius called out, "Now!"

The surrounding men surged forward, battering the rebel forces now from both sides as they let out loud war cries of fury. Gaius himself met the dark-eyed man before him with a savage howl, spinning his blade up, around, and underneath the man's chin. He adroitly avoided the man's spear thrust in the process as he lurched to the right, its tip barely skimming his earlobe.

He caught the shaft with one hand and yanked his opponent forward, drawing the man in on the tip of his blade. The insurgent dropped like a rock.

Gaius spun around to see Marcus doing battle with an over-sized man dual-wielding mallets in his beefy, muscle-corded arms.

Marcus looked to be holding his own, but as Gaius glanced over, the boy's foot slipped on the edge of an unseen rock and he stumbled backward. He landed flat, the air knocked out of his lungs as he stared up in horror at the downward arc of a mallet aimed straight for his head.

Gaius lunged toward them but knew with a sinking sensation that he was much too far away.

Then a much smaller figure barreled into the man, forcing him to lurch sideways but nearly losing his own footing in the process. The figure stumbled but steadied himself, turning to face the furious man.

Diolun Maher.

Sword raised and at the ready, Diolun blocked the man's first downward swing but missed the meaty fist that flew up to pummel him in the stomach.

He doubled over, bile spilling from his throat, but somehow kept hold of his blade. By then, Gaius had reached them and shouted to draw the insurrectionist's attention away from the two boys. As the man's beady little eyes turned to face him, Gaius blocked another overhead swing of the mallet, moving with the momentum so that the man spun around, perfectly poised for Gaius to plunge his sword deep into the beefy man's belly.

Turning away, Gaius looked down into the wide-eyed gaze of the two young Tiros. Diolun, still coughing, stared up at him in gratitude, while Marcus couldn't tear his eyes away from the uplander comrade who'd saved him, his tormentee turned deliverer.

"W-why? Why did you . . . ?"

"Forget it," Diolun said, still heaving. "You'd have done the same."

Gaius thought Marcus looked unsure as to this fact, but Gaius dragged him to his feet anyway.

"There's no time," he barked. "Fight your way through. We'll rally at the stone building in the center of the yard."

The sound of a female shriek drew his attention.

Braína.

He looked around desperately for her flaxen braids but could see nothing through the mass of lurching bodies.

"Go!" he yelled at the two boys, pushing them toward the building.

He took off at a run, not bothering to see whether the boys obeyed him. *I have to find her*, he thought desperately.

Gaius couldn't say how many men he cut through trying to reach his second-in-command, searching for her and her cohort.

He finally found her in the northeast corner, and she seemed to be single-handedly fighting off half a dozen men simultaneously.

As Gaius ran toward her, he watched as she blocked an undercut to the side, grappling with the man's wrist.

"To me!" he called.

Her eyes met his, and she swiftly kneed the man in the gut, spinning him around to receive Gaius's blade through the neck. Gurgling, the man dropped to the ground.

Gaius yanked his sword free and turned to face the next assailant.

"Seems you got yourself into a bit of trouble here," he commented to Braína mildly. The two of them were now back-to-back, fending off incoming attacks from both sides.

She laughed without mirth. "Never. As I recall, I was comin' to save *your* sorry arse, sir."

They sprung apart as a downward swing threatened to sever them. Gaius blocked it, swiftly disarming the man and clobbering him over the head with the hilt of his sword.

"I don't know if I'd use the word 'save,' Decius. Perhaps 'support' or 'reinforce.'"

Braína cackled. "Nah, I like 'save' just fine, sir."

She grunted as she took a boot to the gut but kept her balance and spun out of the way to avoid a second blow. She kicked her assailant in the back, piercing him through the spine with her blade.

The five men remaining looked warily between the two of them, seemingly unwilling to advance farther.

Shoulder to shoulder, Gaius and Braína brandished their weapons, offering their most threatening grins.

The men turned and ran for the seaport, and the two of them let out audible sighs of relief, slumping slightly in exhaustion.

"So, twenty men, did you say, sir?" Braína asked, hands on knees as she paused to catch her breath.

Gaius scowled at her before turning to survey the remaining fighters. The insurrectionists were quickly dwindling, as were their own Bellatori numbers.

"I'll throttle whatever scout gave such a piss-poor report," he growled. "Still, we've got a job to do."

Braína nodded, stooping to wipe the blood from her blade.

"Where to, sir?"

"That central stone building, it matches the description of the headquarters. If we're lucky, they didn't have time to burn the evidence."

CHAPTER

SEVEN

As they rounded the row of huts before the stone headquarters at the encampment's center, the sound of shouting and cries of outrage made them freeze. Then, rushing forward, they emerged into the clearing to find an injured Sergius Tullius, blood pouring from a wound to his leg, and a handful of Bellators fighting back a slowly advancing group of rebels. *Likely left behind to destroy any evidence*, Gaius thought. Running toward them with blades unsheathed, Gaius and Braína caught the rebels from behind and began cutting their way through until they reached the embattled Bellators. Panicking at the sudden attack from all sides, the rebels who remained standing turned then and made for the jungle. Turning to the group of Bellators, Gaius quickly took stock.

"Everyone all right?"

Sergius Tullius said nothing but with a barely audible moan sank slowly down the stone wall he'd moved to lean against. Braína quickly knelt beside the shaking Tullius and quickly undid her belt, looping it around his leg as high as she could above the injury and cinching it tight.

"You need a healer," she said perfunctorily, and Gaius saw her eyeing Tullius's white-faced grimace. "And soon."

"I-I'll be fine," the older man grunted, trying and failing to rise from the ground.

"You most certainly will not," Braína informed him, gesturing for two waiting Bellators to help her lift him. "Get him back to the garrison," she ordered. "See to it the camp surgeon has a good look at him."

Tullius conceded to allow himself to be helped up, but Gaius saw him level on Braína a long, furrowed look before murmuring, "Thank you, Decius."

Braína held his gaze for a long moment before finally nodding. "See to your wounds, Sergius. You fought well today. I'd see you back on your feet as soon as you're able."

Gaius fought back the smile that threatened but said nothing, merely following his second-in-command into the stone headquarters.

INSIDE, they found Diolun and Marcus had already started organizing the documents, securing them in the trunks the rebels had so conveniently left for them.

"Anything useful, boys?" Gaius asked, moving to shuffle through a stack of paperwork.

Diolun's face turned red, and he stammered something about not taking the time to read through them. Gaius cursed his own slipup. Of course the boy probably couldn't read.

Marcus, clearly seeing Diolun's discomfort, quickly interjected, "I said I'd organize them, sir. Seems to me to be mostly requisition reports, account balances for shipping, and the like. No letters or anything calling for direct revolt, I'm afraid."

Gaius eyed him quizzically.

Interesting turn of events, he thought. The downlander bully sticking up for his uplander comrade. *Well, I'd hope saving someone's life would foster some degree of loyalty*, he thought with satisfaction.

However, the reality of Marcus's words quickly dimmed his blooming optimism. No letters? Nothing to prove the rebels' intentions? Well, at least the requisition and shipping reports were something. Besides, there might be more in the chests that the boys hadn't gotten to. He'd take a look once the lot of them were clear of the place.

Braína frowned at him. "Sir, it might be worth checkin' down at the port. I saw a ship still in its moorin's as we approached. Could be they had letters or reports due to be sent out."

Gaius nodded. "Good thought. You boys stay here and ready all these for transport. We'll take a group of Tiros down to the port. I'm sure the villagers have heard what's happened. Any rebel survivors will have fled to the ship by now."

Braína nodded and followed him outside. Gaius summoned all the Bellators he could find, save two, whom he sent to look for the wounded man he'd had to leave at the outset of the fight. He instructed them to bring the wounded Bellator here to the rendezvous point and provide whatever medical aid they could. Gaius wasn't sure if the boy had survived. But if he was lucky, the enemy would have been distracted by the bulk of the attack and left him well enough alone.

Summoning Braína and the others, Gaius led the way toward the road leading to the port and the village that surrounded it.

"Keep on your guard," he ordered the others, drawing his own blade. "There's no telling what rebels may be lying in wait."

Braína nodded, checking behind her to make sure the younger Tiros were following their lead.

As Gaius made his way along the path, he kept as quiet as he could while rounding each corner of the path. His vision was obscured by the dense overgrowth of jungle flora, and every step threatened mishap from the curling vines and massive roots that sprung up from the moist earth.

The jungle was silent, and a sense of unease settled on Gaius. As they neared the last bend in the path, he paused, gesturing for the others to halt behind him. He smelled the air, nostrils flaring.

The familiar scent of charred wood and cooked meat wafted around them.

With a sudden surge of panic, he picked up their pace and rounded the last curve in a rush, only to freeze at the sight before them.

From their earlier visit to the tiny fishing village that surrounded the smuggling port, Gaius guessed that it housed at least two dozen families, the wives and children of fishermen who used the port for their legitimate shipping business. Yet from what his eyes could see, there was nothing but fire and the crumbling remains of once well-built wooden structures.

Beside him, Braína inhaled sharply, letting out the air in a thin hiss.

"Who did this?" she asked.

Gaius shook his head, feeling his bones heavy with weariness.

"The rebels?" one of the Tiros piped up.

Gaius said nothing, but inside he doubted it. Most of the rebels were native to the Southern Shield. What reason could they have for destroying the homes of their friends and neighbors?

No, someone else did this.

Gaius said nothing, though, merely motioning the others forward. They moved uneasily through the charred remains of the village, pausing at each home to check for survivors. But as time went on and the charred remains accumulated, they lost more and more hope.

"They can't all be *gone*," Braína murmured. "Surely some of them escaped."

Gaius merely shook his head, thinking of the kind woman painting scenes of spirit-binders onto bark cloth, the one who'd warned that they'd bring only chaos with them. Turned out she'd been correct.

Just then, they broke through the dense underbrush to reveal the sandy beach sloping down to the port below. And, as if summoned by Braína's words, they could hear the low wails and cries of a crowd of women and children huddled by the water's edge, clinging to its shores as if for safety from the flames. Gaius felt a solid stone settle in the pit of his stomach, and the feeling quickly turned to outright nausea as he turned to see the other occupants of the beach.

A crowd of Bellators swarmed along the beach, carrying chests and unloading cargo from the burnt-out remains of the smugglers' ship. Gaius could see the Bellatori ship moored farther out to sea, with smaller boats rowing to and from it laden with the spoils of conquest.

Amid the swirl of red uniforms, Gaius could see a single plumed helm. He made for it, his weariness suddenly buoyed by a renewed sense of fury.

When he was mere paces away, the man turned to reveal the sneering face of Millus Szerio.

"You," Gaius breathed, eyes fixed on the man's beady-eyed face.

"Ah, Centus Flavius. Odd I should find you here. The western front too much for you, then?"

"Hardly, sir. Was it too much for *you*?"

Szerio's face hardened, his mouth settling into a thin line. He ignored the question and instead leveled one of his own. "I was told you would be clearing the encampment. I take it you were successful?"

"It is secured," Gaius said through gritted teeth.

"Good, good. So I take it you were able to find evidence of the rebels' activities?"

"No," he said thinly. "Only shipping manifestos and requisition reports, nothing damning."

Szerio had already turned away, as if suddenly losing interest in the conversation. "Ah, pity. Well, hopefully the evidence my men find on their ship will be more helpful for us. Never mind, Centus. I'm sure you did your best."

Gaius had to bite back the icy rage that coursed through his veins, tamping it down lest he actually throttle this stout little man before getting the information he needed.

"And what, *sir*, happened to the village? From the last scouting reports, it was still standing. My orders were to leave it untouched."

"Were they? Well, my orders were to root out insurrection. The villagers were unwilling to give up their rebel leaders, so we were forced to root them out ourselves."

"By burning and pillaging an innocent village?" Gaius could feel his scalp prickling and his neck burning hot.

"My dear Centus, these are enemies of the state, seeking to subvert the Marian crown. They are smugglers, insurrectionists, and rebels of all sorts. Far from *innocent*, as you say."

"There were women and children, noncombatants, in that village," Gaius said, barely keeping hold of the rage that coursed through him.

"Yes, and as you can see, they're all over there, perfectly safe."

"*Some* are safe. We passed the corpses of the less lucky on our way here!" Gaius's hands had balled into fists by this point, and he cheerfully imagined socking Szerio in the nose with one of them. "They have no homes, no livelihood. These people will starve, Szerio, because of you and your damn belligerence."

"Well, then, they should not have taken up with insurrectionists," Szerio spat, eyes narrowing to slits. "You have your orders, *Centus*, and I have mine."

Szerio paused, waiting to see if Gaius would challenge him further. He certainly wanted to, would have given anything to grind this fat arsehole's face into the mud. He could barely see straight and was about to respond angrily that the conversation was in no way over, when Braína's cool hand on his arm made him pause. The warning look in her eye was enough to tether him, dulling the rage that threatened to overwhelm him, even if it was far from dissipated.

Clearly satisfied that he'd won the argument, Szerio continued, "Now, if you'd care to join me, we need to make a report as to the state of our operations here."

"Very well, *sir*."

Gaius would follow this man. He was, after all, a superior officer. But there was no way in hell that Gaius was not reporting Szerio's excesses directly to high command. Of *that*, he could be certain.

~

GAIUS FOLLOWED Szerio as he made his way among the rows of chests that had been off-loaded from the smugglers' ship. With each pause that Szerio made to check the contents and annotate his own observations, Gaius felt his weariness grow. It was just after dawn, and he'd been up the entire night. He was also eager to check on his own men, who he'd left back in the encampment. He needed to account for his own losses, and yet here he was following this pompous Millus around as he catalogued his victories. The absurdity of it disgusted him.

It was when they'd moved on to the second row of chests that Gaius spotted the young Tiro. The red robe of the Bellatorio fluttered around him, identifying him as such. But there was just something about him that made Gaius uneasy.

Maybe it was the boy's steely eyes as he watched Millus Szerio, or the stiffness with which he stood at attention, but somehow *wrongly*. Or maybe it was—there! There it was. It was the boy's hair. It hung in lanky strands that stretched down to his jaw, well out of regulation for Bellators.

Gaius furrowed his brows, about to make an on-the-spot correction, when the boy's eyes lit on him and he froze.

Maybe he could see his antagonism, or maybe it was merely the realization that he'd been seen. But it was enough.

Leaping forward, the boy brandished his blade, aimed in an upward swing toward the turned back of Millus Szerio. Gaius lunged forward to grab him, not even thinking to unsheathe his only weapon. It all happened too quickly.

The cold bite of steel cut through him.

Then everything went dark.

CHAPTER

EIGHT

Two Months Later

In the regal corridors of the city garrison of Crîd Eálas, Gaius waited with barely muted frustration. He'd been there for nearly an hour now, seeking an audience with Imperator Lanus. They'd offered to reschedule, to have him return another day. But Gaius knew better than to trust the creaking cogwheels of bureaucracy to get him the audience he required. No, this meeting was long overdue. Leaning against the cold stone walls, Gaius eased his weight off of his left leg. He gripped the walking stick that he'd grudgingly conceded to in one viselike hand as the throbbing continued unabated.

It had been two months since the debacle in Tibolé. Their operations had found evidence of smuggling but not of armed insurrection. Once more, Gaius had a bone to pick with Imperator Lanus, not only for the inaccurate scouting report that had cost him the lives of three of his men but also in the heavy-handed extremism that Millus Szerio had allowed to run rampant, destroying the local village without regard to life or property. No amount of pain would stop him from seeking his appeal.

After the failed assassination attempt on Szerio himself, Gaius

48

had woken in excruciating pain to find that his left leg had been sliced from ankle to hip by the would-be assassin. He'd later been told that Braína had been the one to leap forward, her decisive parry saving him from being well and truly skewered, all for the sake of Szerio.

Still, by the time he'd awoken, they'd feared it would not be enough to save his leg. The surgeon had offered to simply amputate, explaining that the pain and deformity that accompany such a wound would likely not be worth the hassle and that he would make better use of a well-fitted stump. Gaius had threatened to slit the man's throat if he came near him, and one look at Braína's steely gaze had been enough to convince the surgeon his skills were more needed elsewhere. Gaius hadn't seen that particular medical professional since.

In his weeks in the hospital ward, he'd written many letters to Lanus, making use of the endless hours that stretched before him with no sign of abating. Finally, when he was well enough to hobble about on a cane, his left leg barely able to flex at the knee, he told Braína that he had to go.

"And you think it will do much good?" she'd asked. "If Lanus won't reply to you now, what makes you think—"

"I'll make him answer for this. I'll show up at his own damn villa if I have to."

Braína had said nothing to that, merely raised her hands in mock surrender. Gaius knew he was being unreasonable. But between the pain in his leg and the sharper pain of the Bellatorio dreams he could feel slipping away, he wasn't much in the mood for reason.

Braína had eyed him warily then. "I don't know about this, sir. I don't trust—"

"*I'm* the one that got us into this, Erin. I'm the one who took Lanus up on his offer. I'm as much to blame as anyone, but I'll be damned if there aren't consequences for whatever went wrong here."

Braína had glanced at him, surprised. He rarely used her first name. It was technically a breach of military decorum to do so. But over the previous weeks, he'd trusted only her to tend to his leg, leveling a threatening scowl at all else who ventured near it. She'd teased him at first but in the end had taken over all medical duties without a second thought.

The friendship the two of them had formed over two years of shared service had quickly morphed into a companionship bordering on devotion. He owed her, Gaius knew, owed her more than anyone.

"Fine," Braína said. "I'll ready my things. There's a ship heading out at first light. We can leave then."

"No," Gaius said firmly. The word came out sharper than intended.

A hurt expression flashed across her face, and he quickly clarified.

"I need you here," he said more gently. "I need you to look after the men. Two of them are still in hospital, and I need someone I trust to keep me informed as to *his* activities."

In the time Gaius had been in the hospital, Szerio had taken over every aspect of Bellatori operations on Tibolé, setting up a full occupation of the small island and paying little mind to the wishes of its inhabitants. Word of his harsh policies and even harsher punishments had reached even Gaius's ears as he lay in sick bay. He did not trust that man with a dog, let alone Gaius's own Bellators, the ones who had trusted him and who he'd led directly into this cockamamie mess.

Gaius shook his head again. "No, I need you here to keep an eye on Szerio, Erin. I don't trust him, and I don't trust he won't take every opportunity to turn this whole mess into something for his own personal gain."

Braína frowned, then nodded hesitantly. "Gaius, sir, are you sure you want to do this?"

Gaius rubbed a hand across face, weariness eating at his very bones. "I have to do this. It's my responsibility."

"Not everything is your responsibility, sir."

Gaius smiled wanly at her. "This is."

~

As Gaius thought back to this last conversation he'd had with Braína, he felt his brows knit together. He'd had no word from her since leaving the Southern Shield over two weeks prior. He'd heard that a tropical storm had briefly halted communications, but this was yet another thing to add to his growing list of concerns, and yet another reason that he refused to be put off another day.

The sound of voices shook Gaius from his reverie, and he straightened off the wall with difficulty. He manually adjusted his leg so that it could fully bear his weight, even as he leaned heavily on his cane.

The door to Lanus's offices opened, and two men emerged, with the Imperator close behind. They were dressed in opulent robes of fuchsia and teal, and the scent of their perfumed skin wafted before them, making Gaius's nose curl in disgust.

"A pleasure as always, Cyprian."

"Ah, my dear Quintus, the pleasure is most assuredly mine." Imperator Lanus smiled jovially as he shook hands with the two men. "I do hope we'll have the chance to work even more closely together in the future."

"Well, you do know what they say," the one he'd called Quintus replied, grinning jocularly at his friend. "The Shield is nothing if not lucrative."

The three of them laughed, although Gaius couldn't have said exactly what made the joke funny. Yet there was something about them, Gaius thought as he watched them saunter down the hall, that made him uneasy. Perhaps it was their confidence, their status, so easily assumed and yet no doubt undefended and unearned, that put his teeth on edge.

After a moment spent waving after his friends, Lanus turned suddenly to Gaius.

"Why, Centus Flavius! I'm so sorry, did we have an appointment?"

Gaius pulled himself to the highest height he could, twitching his chin upward slightly as he stared Lanus down. "We did, sir. Your assistant tried to reschedule, but I insisted that I must see you today."

Lanus blinked but showed no sign of annoyance, merely gesturing for Gaius to follow him into the offices.

Heaving himself forward, Gaius lumbered through the doorway, managing not to wince despite the fire that coursed up his leg with every step. Inside, Gaius was surprised to find that the Spartan accommodations that Lanus had so preferred while touring the western front were a world away from the opulence before him.

Lanus's offices were lavishly decorated with gold brocade draped as wall hangings and priceless statuary decorating the alcoves. Lanus himself sat behind a great wooden desk that gleamed with recent polishing.

"So, Centus Flavius, please make yourself comfortable."

Gaius complied, lumbering toward the desk and easing himself into the chair, his left leg kept ramrod straight before him as he leveled his gaze at the Imperator.

"I was certainly sorry to hear of your injury, Centus," Lanus continued, "although by all accounts it was gallantly won, saving a superior officer from a would-be assassin. Millus Szerio has put you in for a commendation."

"As he should," Gaius murmured, "along with *his* resignation."

"What was that?" Lanus inquired, sounding curious but still not lifting his eyes from the paper he was scribbling away on.

"Nothing, sir," Gaius replied. He knew that disparaging comments would not help him with what he had to do.

"All right, well, what can I help you with today, Centus?"

"Sir, I'm here to provide you with my report of our operations in Tibolé."

"I already received your report, Centus. I assure you, it was very thorough and well-documented. I took no issue with it."

Gaius tried to squash the rising impatience that bloomed in his chest, threatening to make his heart race and his words trip over themselves. "Thank you, sir. But with all due respect, I never received your response."

"And what sort of response were you seeking, Centus?"

Gaius deliberately slowed his words, his nostrils flaring against a rising tide of anger. "Sir, in my report, I thoroughly documented how we were given incorrect intelligence that directly led to the death of three of my men and the critical injury of two others."

"Centus, as I'm sure you of all people are aware, scouting reports are notoriously incomplete and inaccurate. It is an unfortunate byproduct of the Fog of War, I'm afraid. Or would you see every scout flogged for inaccuracy?"

Gaius gritted his teeth. "Of course not, sir."

"Good, then—"

"But sir, there is still the issue of Millus Szerio's actions!"

Lanus paused and for the first time looked up from his notes, leveling Gaius with a piercing gaze. "And what actions would those be, Centus?"

Gaius could only stare at him. "He looted and pillaged an entire village, sir. Men, women, and children who had no connection with the insurrectionists were killed or forced from their homes, which were then destroyed. They've completely lost their livelihood and are now living under occupation!"

Lanus's eyes narrowed further. "Centus, as I'm sure Millus Szerio explained to you, the villagers were hardly innocent. In truth, they were hiding insurrectionists within their very ranks. What's more, they refused to cooperate with the crown, denying a direct order from a Bellatori leader. Whatever lives were lost were done so in outright insurrection. Whatever property seized was done so as due penalty for undermining the crown's authority."

Gaius stared at him, not believing his ears. Was this the same man who had spoken to him about duty and justice? He'd applauded him for putting the well-being of his people above all else. And here he was now openly discussing the slaughter of innocents in service to crown and country. Gaius thought he might be sick.

"Besides, Centus. I have to say, your operations were a rousing success! The smuggling operations were likely permanently disrupted, and no one in the Southern Shield will ever again plot insurrection without due regard for the consequences."

A sudden thought occurred to Gaius, and he quickly pushed it aside, the disgust in the idea too much to bear. But it refused to be silenced, and with an unsteady breath, Gaius brought forth the question. "Who were those men, sir? The ones that arrived just before I did. They looked, well, they looked patrician."

For the first time, Gaius saw what he thought was a glint of panic in Lanus's eye, but it disappeared just as quickly with a brush of the Imperator's hand.

"Old friends of mine, and yes, they've done quite well for themselves in the business world, I suppose."

A cold stone settled in Gaius's stomach. He thought about retreating, but he'd come too far for such a thing now. "And, may I ask, what type of business do they engage in, sir?"

Lanus's eyes narrowed once more. "Why?"

Gaius shrugged, leaning forward slightly as he stared unblinking into Lanus's eyes. "They just seem . . . *well-off*."

"Any number of things, Centus: salt, paper, incense, furs, and . . ." Lanus paused here, leveling Gaius with a challenging stare, daring him to react to what they both knew was coming. "Tellurium."

A wave of nausea washed over Gaius as he stared at the man he'd once considered a mentor. *Tellurium,* the precious metal and chief export of the Southern Shield. The weight of what he'd done threatened to crash over him, and he staggered beneath it. Of course, powerful men in the capital would wish to see smuggling in the Southern Shield rooted out—anything that cut into their own coffers.

"There never were insurrectionists, were there, sir?"

Lanus shrugged. "There have *always* been insurrectionists in the Southern Shield, Gaius. We conquered their country. Even two hundred years on, they still haven't forgiven us."

Gaius blew out in exasperation, shaking his head. "And why should they, sir? We seem to have proven time and again that we don't give a shit about them or their islands. If you'll excuse me, *sir*, I think that'll be all."

Heaving himself to his feet, he shuffled toward the door, struggling to keep his balance as his hands shook with fury, barely holding onto the cane he clutched for support.

"Oh, and Gaius," came the call from behind, just as his hand gripped the doorknob, "I don't think I need to tell you the importance of keeping such information 'need-to-know,' purely for good order and discipline, you understand."

Gaius closed his eyes, willing himself to breathe steadily. His eyes snapped open and a wave of calm suddenly washed over him. He knew what he had to do.

"I don't think that will be a problem, sir," he said, voice sounding cool and collected even to his own ears. "You'll have my resignation on your desk by midmorning."

And with that, he threw open the door and strode out, suddenly feeling more in control of his life than he had in half a decade.

CHAPTER

NINE

"I can't do it anymore, Aelianna, I just can't. I have to resign!"

Gaius's pacing had taken on a life of its own, the throbbing that reverberated through his leg with each step nothing compared to the fury that pulsed in his veins.

"Take a breath, Gaius. You don't have to decide tonight."

"I sure as hell do. I told him as much, the bastard. He's in on it, you know," Gaius blurted, rounding on her and brandishing a finger like a weapon. "He may think I don't know Tellurium merchants when I see them. He'd be wrong! The smell of them, you can practically taste the human suffering they peddle. Everyone knows a Tellurium mine is the fastest way to an ignoble death. Here on the mainland, it's a fate worthy only of prisoners and convicts. But in the Shield, no, they can get away with whatever they want!"

"I'm well aware of what goes on in a Tellurium mine, Gaius." An icy note had crept into Aelianna's voice, and Gaius stared at her, mouth suddenly the consistency of sawdust.

"Aelianna, I—I'm so sorry. Here I am running my mouth like a fool. How could I—"

She raised a hand, silencing his sputtering apologies. "It's

56

nothing, Gaius," she said, a sudden weariness dripping from every syllable. "It was a long time ago."

Gaius cursed his own idiocy. How could he have forgotten that Aelianna's own brother had been sentenced to hard labor in a Tellurium mine nearly a decade before? Left to fend for herself on the harsh streets of Crîd Eálas, not yet fifteen and with no family or prospects to think of, it was little wonder she'd turned to the only industry that promised young girls a livable wage and upward mobility. She hadn't seen her brother since, had had no word whether he'd lived or died. She rarely spoke of him, but Gaius knew that he occupied the glimmer of sadness that filled her face in quiet moments when she thought herself unseen.

"It's not nothing, Aelianna. I should never have—"

She raised her hand again, mouth pressed into a thin line, and Gaius knew it was time to move past this particular subject.

"The question, Gaius, is what will you do now?"

Gaius rubbed a callused hand across his face, every sinew of his body suddenly aching with exhaustion. "What can I do?"

A look of annoyance flashed across her face. "You could go to high command, tell them what happened."

Gaius was shaking his head before she'd even finished. "I have no proof. We documented the entire operation, scouting reports accounted for and suspicion of rebel activity reported. As far as the Bellatorio is concerned, there's nothing to suggest that Lanus did anything improper. Whatever arrangements he made with the Tellurium merchants, I can't imagine he left a paper trail."

Aelianna's mouth was set in a thin line, and she gave him a hard look. "Then focus on what you can prove, Gaius. There were clearly excesses taken on Tibolé. Even if there had been suspicion of rebel activity, you said yourself that that wouldn't justify pillaging an entire village."

Gaius nodded, jaw tightening. "You're right. And that's exactly what I'll state as the basis for my resignation."

Aelianna's mouth twisted slightly and her brow furrowed.

"And if they don't listen to you? If they do nothing with the information you've given them?"

"Then I'll take it to the people, post it in the forums, and give the news to the criers. I'll make it known to everyone how the Bellatorio, an ancient institution meant to serve the Lorenan people, is actually in bed with wealthy merchants."

Aelianna nodded, but Gaius's dogged determination was not matched in the expression she wore. She paused, weighing her words. "Gaius, you know I hate what's happened as much as anyone, more even, but I worry that if you do this, you won't be safe in Loren anymore."

Gaius stared at her, uncomprehending. "Why would that be?"

"Gaius, you think they'll allow you to smear their name with no consequences?" She shook her head. "I know you trust them—"

"I'd trust them with my life, Aelianna." Gaius threw her a reproachful look. "There may be a few rotten apples, but my family has served the Bellatorio nobly for *centuries*. Sure, Lanus and his cronies are well connected, but once the truth is made known publicly, high command will see to it that there are due consequences for all involved."

Aelianna pursed her lips. She looked like she wanted to argue further, when they were interrupted by a brisk knock on the door. Shooting Gaius one more concerned look, Aelianna called, "Enter!"

A Bellatori messenger boy entered, looking about the rooms hesitantly. His eyes lit up when they landed on Gaius, and he snapped to attention. "Sir! Message for you!"

Gaius sighed. "From high command?"

This had to be the official censure he'd been expecting, stemming no doubt from his rudeness toward Lanus. He stepped forward, hand outstretched.

"No, sir," the boy piped up, passing him the letter. Gaius could see that it was stamped with a familiar seal. "From the Southern Shield."

Eagerly, Gaius took it and cracked the seal in one swift motion. *Word from Braína,* he thought, *at last.*

He had to scan the letter's contents twice for the reality of her words to sink in. He sagged against the nearest table, arm barely holding his weight as his legs threatened to give out. *No*, he thought, *this can't be happening.*

Seeing his suddenly ashen face, Aelianna quickly ushered the boy out.

"—find the cook downstairs, tell her I sent you for a warm meal and a drink to lift your spirits. There's a good lad." The boy looked back at Gaius hesitantly but allowed himself to be excused.

"You'll tell the Centus I'm available for a return message?" he murmured to her. "Anyfing he needs. My bruvva's in his unit, swears he saved his life."

Aelianna nodded, brows knit together. "Of course, just wait downstairs, there's a good lad."

The door closed and Aelianna was at his side in a moment, hands clasped around his suddenly freezing fingers as her eyes searched his face. "What is it, Gaius? What's happened?"

"They're gone," he said simply. "They're all gone."

Dear Sir,

I pray this finds you well. And I beg your pardon for not writing sooner; for weeks I could not find the words. But Gaius, I must tell you now of the awful tragedy that has struck our camp.

In the first few days, we thought it only a mild illness, perhaps transmitted in the water or by contaminated meat. Nearly a handful of the young Tiros came down with it. Their own vomiting and dysentery may have left them wishing for death, but in truth they should have come through it just fine. We assumed it was only food or water contamination. But then the fever set in.

The locals call it the wasting disease, but our camp surgeon, before he succumbed to the disease himself, called it the blood sickness. I prayed for days he was wrong, but the facts of the matter couldn't be denied. Just as the tales say, it comes every three days, waxing and waning like the moon itself.

The lads would writhe in their beds, soaked to the bone with sweat, yet shivering as if Séiro himself had caught hold of them. I regret to say that we lost three in the first week. We tried to isolate them, sir, per the instructions of the camp surgeon, just in case it was not food that had caused it. But I'm afraid we were too late.

In the second week, ten Tiros came down with it, and their symptoms were worse than the first ones afflicted. We lost half, and another from the first batch when his fever returned with a vengeance. It was then that I put pen to paper to write to you, Gaius, to inform you of all that had happened.

But then the rest of us fell ill. Even as I sit here, writing now, sir, my teeth chatter and my bones ache. The fever comes and goes, and when it is here, I barely have the strength to lift my head from the bed. Every day I live in fear of the return of the dreaded fever. I wake in the middle of the night to the sound of men screaming as they clutch at limbs that have turned alabaster white as their blood slows to a crawl from within.

For most, it fades within a few minutes, with life returning to the limb. But for some, it never does. When they pass out from the pain of it, we call for the surgeon, who makes quick work of the wasted limb, desperate that it should not become infected and hasten the poor lad to his death.

Even as I write, my own fingers stiffen and cramp, and every twinge of pain is a stab to the heart as I fear what may come next. It's for this reason that I have resolved to write to you, while I still can.

I beg you not to return, Gaius. I know that the path you have set yourself on is one of importance, a quest for justice for the men we've lost and the lives that have been ruined because of frank failures of leadership. And I know that as you read this, you will feel compelled to come at once. But I beg you, Gaius, there is nothing you can do here. None of us wishes to see our leader succumb to such as this. I only write now so as to send word and preserve a record for what has happened so that you may not wonder.

In case I do not see you again, Gaius, I must tell you it has been the honor of my life to serve under you. I never thought the military life had much for me, never thought I'd make a good Decius. But being your second-in-command, sir, has been an honor and a privilege. I have learned so much from witnessing your leadership. My only regret is that I never got the chance to implement the lessons you taught me for myself.

The last time I saw you, we parted on good terms. And I like to think I will end this life not only as your comrade but as your friend as well.

Respectfully and Dutifully,

Decius Erin Braína, Fourth Centurium of the Western Imperium

AT THE SIGHT of Gaius's pale face, Aelianna immediately reached for his hands. "Tell me," she said. "What's happened?"

He shook his head mutely, passing her the letter, which his trembling fingers had unknowingly crumpled into a ball. She quickly scanned the words and let out a small gasp.

When she was finished, her eyes found his, soft with sympathy. She reached for his arm. "I'm so sorry, Gaius. I can't imagine what you're going through. If one of my girls . . . I don't know what I would do."

Gaius rubbed his eyes with one hand, shaking his head. "I can't believe I wasn't there. I can't believe I *left* them. And for what? For a Bellatorio that didn't even listen to me? For a corrupt—" His voice croaked off, unable to continue. Instead, he merely stooped and began gathering up his things.

"What are you doing?" Aelianna asked.

He glanced over at her, still mentally running through the calculus of lists and accommodations he'd need to make. "What do you mean?"

"Where are you going?"

"To the Southern Shield," he said offhandedly, mentally calculating how long it would take him to reach the dockyards and charter a ship.

"Gaius, stop!"

For the first time, he looked up from his efforts, eyebrows raised to meet Aelianna's furious glare. What on earth was she upset about? Hadn't she read the letter? His unit had been decimated. What else could he do but find them and try to pick up the pieces?

"You can't seriously be thinking of traveling all the way to the Southern Shield," she began. "What exactly do you think you'll be able to do there?"

"I'll be with my *men*," he said, a little too sharply. "Isn't that enough?"

"Gaius, you've *barely* recovered from your wounds." Aelianna's voice had taken on a pleading note. "You won't survive the blood sickness. There is *nothing* more you can do for them!"

Gaius's eyes narrowed and his jaw tightened. "What, exactly, are you suggesting?"

Aelianna's eyes searched his, confusion warring with fury behind a thin veneer of civility. "Gaius, I'm suggesting that you continue along the path you set out on. Or have you forgotten about Imperator Lanus's deceit?"

Her words stung, and upon seeing him flinch, Aelianna barreled on. "Resign your post, Gaius. Let the people know what dishonor has occurred. Stop this pointless war before it even begins!"

Gaius closed his eyes, weighing her words. He knew she was right. His blood still boiled at the thought of the pompous Lanus and his willingness to toy with others' lives for his own selfish gain. He deserved to be exposed, deserved the public outrage and political pressure he would face. But Gaius couldn't do it, not anymore.

"The quickest way back to the Southern Shield is by Bellatori ship. I can't afford to resign now, Aelianna. My Bellators need me, and this is too important."

"Can't afford—Gaius! You can't afford *not* to. If you go back now, they will own you. You'll never be able to leave, and you will die in a pointless war—that is, if the sickness doesn't kill you first."

"You know I can't leave them, Aelianna. I'm *responsible*. Hell, I'm the one that got them into this mess! They wouldn't even be in the Southern Shield if it weren't for me and my selfish pursuit of glory."

"They were doing their job, Gaius. It is not your fault that this happened."

Gaius shook his head, the misery evident. "Then whose fault is it?"

"It's no one's fault. These things just happen . . ."

"These things *don't* just happen, Aelianna. The blood sickness follows disaster. It follows war and ruin. It is there because *we* brought it there. We brought it to those people's shores, and my men are suffering because of decisions made that had absolutely *nothing* to do with them. And I . . . Well, I refuse to stand by and leave them to their fate. Braína—" Gaius's voice broke, and he leaned heavily against one bedpost, his left leg throbbing. "She's been a loyal friend, Aelianna."

Aelianna's eyes tightened slightly at the name of Gaius's second-in-command, her lips pressed into a thin line. "I don't doubt that, Gaius. But that letter was sent at least a week ago, if not more. They might . . ." Aelianna paused, her gaze searching. "Gaius, they might not even be—"

"Enough!" Gaius cut in, not able to bear even one word more. Aelianna flinched, and guilt immediately flooded him. He continued, voice soft and pleading, "Aelianna, if it were you, if one of your girls was sick, what would it take for you to not go to her? To not nurse her back to health, caring for her, being with her even in her dying moments? You would owe her that. Just as I owe the men and women who serve under me, who followed me into a pointless conflict that did nothing except fill the coffers of the elite and inflict suffering on the people who live there. That is not why I joined the Bellatorio. And I'll be damned if I will let it keep me from fulfilling my duties as an officer."

Silence hung between them, punctuated only by the creak of the bed frame as Gaius leaned ever more heavily against it.

"And if you die?"

Gaius heard the tremulous note in Aelianna's voice, even over the steel edge to her words. He glanced sharply at her and saw that she was blinking furiously. His anger vanished just as quickly as it had come, and he moved toward her, hand outstretched. She pulled away, hands balled into fists as she glared at him.

"If you insist on doing this, Gaius, do not *expect* me to be here waiting when you come back."

His face went blank as he stared at her. Was she serious? "Aelianna—"

"No! I have spent years waiting for you, Gaius, listening for news after every battle, counting the days until I saw you again. And I accepted it, because it was your duty and I understood that. But I will *not* stand by and watch you throw your life away on some pointless crusade. I know you're angry. I can see you're hurting, and I understand that you feel you failed them, but this. Proves. *Nothing*." She was breathing heavily at this point, and he was about to interject when she continued unabated, "Throwing your life away proves nothing, Gaius, and it certainly does not redeem whatever honors you feel you've lost. It merely begs the question of who your duty is truly to." Her voice became quiet then, and she rubbed roughly at her eyes. "Time after time you've asked me to marry you, Gaius, and each time I've refused. Because I knew that I would never truly hold your heart, not in its entirety. So there you have it, Gaius. You have a choice, and only you can make it."

With that she turned and strode toward the door, yanking it open and holding it wide. She stared him down, not blinking even as the tears streamed down her face. He slowly made his way toward her, pausing in the doorway to glance one more time at her. He searched vainly for the words, the ones he knew she wanted to hear, words that would make it better, that would ease the pain he knew he was causing her. But he couldn't find them. There were no words that he could trade for his honor, for his fealty, for the only duty left for him to perform.

He strode out of the room.

CHAPTER

TEN

The journey back to Tibolé seemed to drag on in Gaius's single-minded determination to reach his men. The seconds ticked by in an agony of uncertainty as he wondered desperately what tragic fate they might all have suffered. And Braína, what of Braína? His relationship with Braína had always been one of professional concern. She was his second-in-command, always there to support and back him up should he need it. *And what did that get her?* he wondered bitterly. *A pointless war, a deadly illness, maybe even—*

He stopped himself before his mind drifted on to the horror of what might happen to her, what might have already happened. They were warriors, all of them, and he knew Braína would face her death bravely. But not like this; it shouldn't have to happen like this.

On the fourth day, the ship finally made landfall off the coast of the island of Tibolé, the largest island in the Southern Shield. Gaius hurriedly moved to gather his belongings as he disembarked the ship. The bustling port town of Albé, where his cohort had landed not two months prior, was desolate, its people hurrying about, eyes downcast, as they avoided stopping within reach of their fellow neighbors. No one knew how the blood sickness spread, but all were careful to avoid outstretched hands, keeping their faces covered by rags to prevent the inhalation of noxious fumes. Gaius disembarked with the cargo and was shocked to see the change in the once lively seaside town. As he made his way wearily through the streets, he clutched his walking stick to aid the limp of his wounded leg.

He hired a wagon to carry him through to the Tibolé garrison, where he'd left the centurium. It was expensive, as the driver had no desire to venture anywhere near the source of the sickness. But upon assurances that he could drop Gaius off a mile or more outside the post, he reluctantly agreed.

The carriage ride wasn't smooth, and Gaius gripped onto the side in pain as it lumbered along, his leg protesting at every lurch and jostle. When they finally reached the designated drop-off location, Gaius thanked the driver and passed him the handful of coins he'd promised.

"No need t'be thanking me tha', lad. Save your thoughts for your friends . . . if they be still livin'."

Gaius grimaced at his words and turned then to make his slow, lurching way to the garrison.

The road was a long one, particularly as he had to limp over and around gnarled tree roots that jutted up from the moist jungle floor. Gaius forced himself on, though, focused on the knowledge that his men needed him. He would reach them, no matter what it took.

As he rounded the final bend in the road, the garrison came sharply into view, and Gaius gaped at the sight. There were no guards posted, and the very gates stood propped open and untended. No noise could be heard, and the acrid stench of decay wafted up from the place. As Gaius approached the gates, he braced himself to be hailed, to be asked on what business he came. But there was nothing.

A mounting sense of dread washed through him as he slipped through the open gate. Was there anyone left? A movement to his left caught his eye, and he turned to see two Bellators, dirty rags wrapped around their faces, hauling a body-shaped bundle between them as they lumbered toward the gate.

Gaius headed for them, wincing slightly as his stiff leg caught on a rock, making him stumble. At his approach, the two figures froze, staring at him in astonishment. Then, lowering their package, they unwrapped the rags from their faces and came to attention, forearms thumping chests in salute. Gaius returned the gesture, seeing immediately that it was in fact Diolun and Marcus.

"Sir! It's good to have you back." It was Marcus who spoke first.

Gaius nodded, scanning the desolate camp. Refuse littered the training yard, and the tents and earth were covered in a thin gray dust. Gaius frowned as he glanced back at the forgotten bundle.

"How many?" he asked.

The boys glanced between each other, looking unsure.

"Must be sixty or so by now, sir," Diolun replied, "last time Decius did an accountin'."

Gaius swallowed hard, then nodded. He'd suspected as much, given Braína's report. Still, to hear it said aloud . . .

"What are you doing with the bodies?" he asked, glancing around in search of a burial mound of some sort.

"Well, sir," Diolun began, grimacing, "there were too many of 'em, especially at the start. So . . . so we had to take to burnin' them, to stop the spread, you see."

Gaius stared at him, dumbfounded. Burn bodies? Looking around again at the fine gray dust that covered the garrison, Gaius felt his stomach turn. He nodded, swallowing the bile that rose unbidden to his throat.

"Where is the Decius, then, lads?" The boys glanced at each other again, shifting nervously as they did so. Fear made Gaius speak more harshly than he felt. "Out with it, then!"

"Sh-she's in her tent, sir, over there." Marcus's voice was soft as he nodded to the far end of the training yard. "She's said no one's coming near, lest they be further exposed."

Jaw clenched, Gaius nodded as he turned in that direction. "Good lads. As you were, then. I'll see to the Decius."

As Gaius made for Braína's tent, he felt himself slow slightly with every step, as if delaying their meeting might in turn delay its outcome. When he finally reached the front flap, he hesitated, steeling himself for whatever might lie inside.

"Braína?" he called.

No response. He shifted slightly, moving his weight off his aching leg.

"Decius Braína?" He thought he heard the rustle of fabric but couldn't be sure. Still, there was no response. Deciding then that this was no time for adherence to decorum, he slowly pushed the tent flap aside.

The inside of the tent was dark, the air thick and damp in its stagnancy. He glanced around and at first thought it was empty. Then a slight movement among the blankets on the small cot made him look again.

His gaze met the hollowed-out eyes of Erin Braína, who stared back at him with a glazed look, as if she could see right through him. Gaius moved toward her then, his mouth going dry at the sight of her skin slick with sweat even as she shivered, the surrounding blankets soaked through and reeking. Her skin was sallow and seemed to cling to her bones, making her appear gaunt and waiflike. Even her usually golden hair seemed brittle and thin as it clung to her sweat-riddled skin. Gaius found her hand in the mass of fabric and squeezed it.

"Y-you came back." Her eyes had cleared slightly, though her voice had the grating sound of sandpaper to his ears.

"Of course I did," he murmured, a lump catching in the back of his throat. He tried to clear it, then gave up. He smiled hesitantly at her. "Though I can't say I love what you've done with the place."

She didn't smile, only shifted slightly, grimacing with the effort. Gaius's smile faded.

"We'll get you through this, Erin," he murmured. "I promise you that."

ELEVEN

Gaius worked as if in a trance, putting the garrison to rights with a fury of intention that left everyone and everything trailing in his wake. There were few able-bodied Bellators remaining, with most dead and the rest holed up in their tents, wracked with fever. Gaius latched onto the remainder with a vengeance, ordering them about with a determination borne of fear and the looming specter of failure.

Gaius himself saw to Braína, not trusting anyone else with her care. He soon had her bed stripped of the soaked linens and, with the help of one of the few other female Bellators, got her cleaned up and changed into new clothing. When he checked in on her later that day, she was propped up and had actually taken in some fluids. Satisfied with this marginal improvement, Gaius then turned to the rest of the camp.

Old Sergius Tullius, in his indomitable way, had of course been stricken with fever before proceeding to make a full recovery. In Braína's absence, he'd fashioned himself Gaius's reserve second-in-command and set about organizing the younger men. The two young Tiros Diolun and Marcus were particularly eager to help in these efforts. With the most recent bodies already seen to, Gaius quickly put them to work sweeping the ash from the camp and scrubbing down the worst of the bodily fluids that had accumulated outside tent flaps during the sickness.

The days that followed saw the privies redug as the old ones were buried and fresh rations sent for from the mainland. Gaius used the rest of the cohort's funds to hire locals willing to brave the sickness and provide extra hands for the needed repairs to the garrison. It was backbreaking work, and Gaius worked side by side with the others, ignoring the protests of his still-stiff leg as he bent to shovel out privies or haul stones on his back. He barely slept and conceded to eat only at the insistence of the others.

By the end of the week, Braína seemed to marginally improve and could even hold brief conversations, despite her continued sallow appearance. After initially berating him for ignoring her recommendation that he not return to the islands under any circumstances, she conceded to offer him grudging thanks for returning anyway.

Gaius could feel himself growing weary, the hard work and lack of sleep combining to imbue a fatigue he had never known, even in the hardest days of any prior campaign. It was in the second week that he nearly collapsed in the midday heat and humidity and was promptly ushered to his tent to rest by a very disgruntled Sergius Tullius.

"We do *not* need you falling ill on us, sir," he growled over Gaius's protests, manhandling him toward his tent. "That's the last thing we need."

Resigned to the older man's logic, Gaius conceded to a brief rest to avoid the worst of the heat.

"Very well, only see to it, Sergius, that—"

"I'll check in on her, sir, rest assured."

Gaius was about to clarify that he'd meant all the currently ill Bellators, but he stopped at Tullius's knowing look. Shaking his head, he decided he was simply too exhausted to argue. Instead, he collapsed onto his cot, allowing himself to be quickly engulfed in the folds of much-denied sleep.

Gaius woke with a start to hands roughly shaking his shoulders. His eyes flew open, hand reaching instinctively toward his hilt, as he met the troubled gaze of Sergius Tullius.

"You must come quick, sir. I'm afraid it's Decius Braína. She's taken a turn for the worse."

~

THE SUN WAS FAR to the west when Gaius staggered from his quarters and lurched across the training field. *How long did I sleep for?* He cursed his willingness to listen to Tullius. He shivered despite the heat and willed his stiff leg to move faster.

Reaching Braína's quarters, Gaius didn't hesitate and instead wrenched open the tent flap and staggering through. He froze in the entrance.

He could hear the whistle of her shallow breathing and stared in horror at her glazed eyes, her brow damp with sweat. The fever had returned.

He immediately knelt by her side, gripping one hand in both of his. "Braína . . . Erin, can you hear me?"

Her head moved slightly at his words, and she made some unintelligible noises in the back of her throat. Eying Tullius suspiciously, Gaius growled, "When did this happen?"

Unfazed by his hostility, Tullius replied, "She took a turn a few hours ago. I sent for the healer woman down in the village, and she brought up some poultices to break the fever."

As if summoned by his words, an elderly islander woman bustled through the door, arms laden with freshly cut herbs. She ignored the two Bellators and instead moved toward the table in the far corner of the tent, where she quickly began cutting and grinding the plants and adding them to a half-prepared salve. When she was done, she passed the cream wordlessly to Tullius, who took it and knelt beside Braína. Scooping the salve onto two fingers, he gently began massaging it onto her chest. His fingers moved gently, pausing every once in a while to hold the salve beneath her nose as she inhaled deeply.

Gaius stared at the older man in surprise. He'd never thought of the gruff Sergius as much for caretaking. And since when did Tullius care so much for Braína, the female uplander promoted above him? Gaius shook his head, supposing that war really did make strange bedfellows.

He was brought back to the present by Braína's low moan, and he quickly squeezed her hand, watching with relief as her eyelids fluttered open.

"Gaius . . ." she murmured, turning her face toward him.

"I'm here," he said, voice rough. "I'm here, Erin."

Her eyes seemed to look right through him, but they finally refocused on his. "D-id you find Lanus?" It took him a moment to realize what she was asking. He'd already told her all that had happened upon his return to the mainland, but she'd clearly forgotten in her fevered haze.

"I did," he said, keeping his voice steady even as he heard her breathing grow shallower. "He's . . . he's taking care of everything. Szerio will be reprimanded, and we're all heading home." He wasn't sure what made him say it. But there was something about the look in Erin's eyes, the fading of her breath, that made it impossible for him to repeat the ugly truth. He was rewarded with her slightly dreamy smile. Ignoring Tullius's questioning looks, Gaius hurried on. "In honor of your service, Decius Braína, I'm recommending you be promoted to Centus. You'll receive your own command, leading your own Bellators. You . . . you've earned it." Gaius heard his voice break, and he tightened his grip on Braína's hand.

She began to speak, and he had to lean close to hear her words, which had faded to almost a whisper. ". . . the honor of my life, serving under you, Gaius. I only wish . . ." Her voice faded, and Gaius shook her shoulder roughly. He knew he should leave her be, knew he should let her rest while she was able, but the panic that blossomed in his chest simply wouldn't allow it. He let out a sigh of relief when her eyelids fluttered back open.

"What, Erin? What do you wish?" Gaius felt more than saw

Tullius quietly move toward the door. He couldn't say when the healer woman had left, but she, too, was gone.

"You always . . . I never wanted to disappoint you, sir."

Gaius made a noise in the back of his throat. "I think we're way past 'sir,' Erin."

She nodded weakly, swallowing before opening her mouth to reply. "I always knew you were hers, Gaius. That there could never be . . ." Her voice trailed off, but Gaius was having a hard time speaking himself just then. He opened his mouth, but no words came out. He couldn't say he was surprised. There was a part of him that had always known what lay between them, all that *could* lie ahead of them. His mind turned to Aelianna, and he pushed the thought away. There'd be time for that later.

"You mean . . . a great deal to me, Erin. You always have." She nodded at his words, smiling sadly at him. Her eyelids had half closed, and her words turned to a mumble, but he managed to just catch the end.

". . . the honor of my life, sir."

And with that, she drifted to sleep. Gaius reluctantly let her go, knowing as surely as he'd ever known anything that they'd not speak again. Rising slightly to hover over her, he gently pressed his lips against her forehead.

"The honor is mine, Decius."

Erin Braína clung on for a few more hours before finally slipping into a deep sleep that she never woke from. When she finally passed, Gaius found himself stumbling from her tent, legs threatening to give way beneath him, buckling under the weight of his sorrow. His chest felt like something was physically tearing into it, and he couldn't speak for fear of the choked sobs that would surely emerge. He leaned heavily against a wooden post as a hand came to rest on his shoulder. He looked through blurred eyes at Sergius

Tullius but found that the older man was himself staring out onto the training field.

Following his gaze, Gaius saw the figures of the two young Tiros. With blunted surprise, he saw that Marcus was on hands and knees, vomiting into the dirt as Diolun leaned over him, hand pressed lightly against his back as he called for help. *There goes another one*, a dark, tortured voice murmured in Gaius's mind, *another one you've failed.*

A wracking chill coursed through his body, and Gaius felt his legs give way as he sank to his knees. His vision swam before him, whether from nausea or tears, he couldn't say. He heaved, but nothing came up, his stomach having been empty for the past day at least. A hand under his arm offered to help him up, but he shook it off, preferring instead the welcoming embrace of the blackness that swam across his vision.

CHAPTER

TWELVE

Three Months Later

Gaius slammed the ceramic mug against the bar top and inhaled sharply through his nose, willing his vision to stop swimming. He closed his eyes, cresting the waves of nausea with a skill honed by weeks of practice, and breathed slower as the sensation faded.

"Eh, you all right there, then, fella?"

Gaius opened one bleary eye to meet the gaze of the red-faced tavern keep, whose eyebrows pressed together so tightly as to appear one long, hairy caterpillar. Gaius snorted, a bit too loudly if one cared about that sort of thing, which he didn't. The tavern keep was clearly incapable of seeing the hilarity of the situation, as he only eyed the ale that sloshed from Gaius's mug with distaste. Gaius waggled a finger at him, jabbing it in his chest as he said, "Haaaven't you heard? I'm a . . . damn war hero!"

"Yeah, yeah, go on then, Mr. Hero, out you get. Don't want none of that here."

Fingers tightened under Gaius's arm, tugging insistently. And suddenly Gaius was up and out of the chair. He rounded on the startled tavern keep and with a howl pummeled him straight in the gut. The man wheezed, doubling over and clutching at his middle as his face turned an even darker shade of crimson.

Gaius just stood there, staring at the man. The fury had faded as quickly as it had come, and he was left in a state of shock, unable to say exactly what had sparked it. The momentary silence that had descended on the pub, fueled by shock as much as anything, suddenly lifted as a half dozen men jumped to their feet and rounded on Gaius, clearly ready to subdue him.

Gaius's jaw clenched as he squared himself off, turning so his back was to the door as he slowly backed away from the menacing jeers. A flash of movement to his left, and Gaius ducked just in time to avoid the goblet that swung through the air, mere inches above him. He turned and sidestepped a beefy dockworker's charge and brought two fists down in a swinging arc across his upper back, sending the man sprawling with a satisfying *thunk*.

The others were advancing now, their jeers turned to cries of indignant outrage as they reached for makeshift weapons from the available cutlery. Gaius reached for the hilt of his sword, only to realize belatedly that he'd lost it in a card game the night before. He cursed his stupidity and prepared himself for the sound beating that was sure to come. He advanced on the men.

"Gaius!"

The sound of the familiar voice caught him up short, and he glanced up to see liquid chocolate eyes staring back at him . . . *Aelianna.*

He felt a meaty fist suddenly connect with his jaw, and then he was staring up at the ceiling, watching as the world tilted at a nauseating angle. He waited for the pierce of steel that he knew would come, that he wanted, even. But there was nothing—only the nausea, the anger, and the pain. Then the world went black.

GAIUS AWOKE to the splash of a bucketful of water across his face, and he sat up with a start. Immediately regretting it, he clasped a hand to his head at a sensation like cold steel piercing his skull. He groaned.

"Serves you right, you buffoon. You're lucky I'm in a good mood, or I'd just as soon have left you for the tavern keep. He'd have been happy to string you up himself, I'm sure."

Gaius blinked blearily, trying and failing to bring her into focus. "What do you want, Aelianna?"

His vision had cleared enough to see that she stood in front of him, arms crossed and jaw clenched, giving him a look that could have wrought iron. "What do I *want*? Not a word for months, and you dare ask me what I want? When I didn't hear from you, I assumed you were still back in the Southern Shield. Quite the surprise, then, when I saw one of your Bellators show up in my parlor one evening and inform me you'd all been back these last six weeks. When I asked where I could find you, they promptly informed me that you'd been off drowning your sorrows in whatever tavern had yet to kick your sorry arse out into the street."

He rubbed his eyes with his fingers and stared blearily up at her. "What do you want me to say, Aelianna?"

"I want you to tell me what happened."

"You know what happened."

She stared at him, nostrils flaring, but he met her look for look. He knew very well that word of the Bellatorio's failings in the Southern Shield had long since reached the mainland, of the sickness that had wiped out two-thirds of their number and halted any further incursions into the islands themselves. What more did she want from him?

"Gaius, why didn't you come to me?"

For the first time, Gaius saw a flash of pain cross her face and felt a corresponding wave of guilt, further adding to that of the nausea he was currently suppressing.

"Aelianna—" He tried to find the words, but none would come. The familiar leaden taste of shame filled his mouth. She waited expectantly. "Aelianna, how could I face you? I failed, I failed at everything. I led the men and women under me to their deaths on a faulty mission that led to the slaughter of innocents and the slow, painful death of hundreds. How could I look you, or anyone else for that matter, in the eye after that? I couldn't even look at *myself*."

He searched her eyes for some sign of understanding, forgiveness even. There was none.

"That's bullshit, Gaius, and you know it." The strength of her words startled him, an anger more vehement than even he'd expected. "I know you, Gaius. You've always put honor and duty above all, but this is self-indulgent, even for you. I'm not about to let you throw away everything you've worked for. There are people depending on you, Gaius, and I will not allow you to let them down."

Gaius glared at her, the throbbing in his head reaching a cadence that threatened to overwhelm his power of speech. "Why not? Why not just leave me here to rot in misery? It's what I deserve. Even you'd admit that."

"Because I'm pregnant, you fool!"

The words came out in a flurry of anger, and Aelianna immediately clamped a hand to her mouth, eyes wide.

Gaius could only stare at her.

"Y-you're *pregnant*?" The word felt waxen in his mouth, and he felt it spill clumsily out. It fell between them, weighty and awkward in its immensity. Now that the wave of nausea had passed, Gaius looked Aelianna over more closely. She'd always been thin and waiflike, but now, beneath the delicate muslin she wore, he could see that she did indeed have the start of a definite bulge. *Pregnant? Could she really be pregnant?*

"I wasn't—" She paused, eying him suspiciously, no doubt rightly concerned he might pass out again. "I wasn't going to tell you until you were more . . . settled. But now you know."

"I—I have nothing to offer you now."

Aelianna rolled her eyes. "You don't think I know that?" When he didn't respond to her teasing tone, she added, more subdued, "Good thing I'm not asking for anything. I meant what I said before, Gaius. I don't need rescuing. I've more than enough savings to take care of myself and this little one." She laid a hand gently across her stomach, thoughtfully, then looked up at Gaius hesitantly. "I could use a partner, though. And preferably a sober one."

Gaius felt his nose burn, and he blinked furiously as he tried to stem the rising tears. His jaw clenched reflexively as Aelianna's eyes looked warmly into his. There was invitation there. But more than that, he saw a lifeline, a way out of his misery and self-loathing.

He swallowed. "I'm half the man I was, half the soldier. I'd be better off leaving the Bellatorio, finding a trade, and doing something useful in life." He caressed his stiff left leg, thinking of the gifts the Southern Shield had left him: a bum leg and the specter of the blood sickness, always watching, waiting for the ideal moment to strike.

Aelianna moved toward him, laying a hand lightly on his cheek. "You're more than enough for me, Gaius. You've had a fall, to be sure. But there's still a place for you here. The Bellatorio is your life; it always has been. You can no more leave it than you can leave your own name. It may not be clear now, but there is a purpose to any fight. And I know that you will find meaning again. You will find your way forward, and someday, Gaius, you will serve Loren proudly again."

Gaius swallowed, thinking about all he'd lost: his centurium, the pride and trust he'd held in the Bellatorio . . . Erin Braína. Gaius squeezed his eyes shut. Erin had told him that not everything was his responsibility—if only he could believe that.

No, he'd see things put to right, as well as he was able. And if that meant returning to the very ranks that had betrayed him, then that's what it meant. His Bellators still needed him, and so did his new family.

Reaching up, he took Aelianna's outstretched hand and let her pull him to his feet.

GAIUS'S STORY CONTINUES IN...

Chaos Looming

Build more than you break.
Heal more than you destroy.
But what if chaos can't be tamed?

Book 1 in The Legion of Pneumos series.

Read on for a sneak peek...

CHAOS LOOMING
CHAPTER ONE

Not for the first time, Keira Altman was suddenly very aware of just how underrated flashlights were, cursing the complete absence of all such useful technology in the realm of Loren. Such revelations weren't limited to times spent creeping toward wooded lodges in the dead of night while trying to *not* impale herself on her sword. There were, in fact, many things she missed about her old world, television and the internet merely first among many. Yet it was moments like these when she became infinitely more appreciative of the mundane miracles that had filled twenty-first-century life in Northern California.

She was just beginning to muse on the glories of ice cream and refrigeration in general when the grim figure leading the cohort fell to his knees, gesturing for them to follow suit. Keira dropped to a crouch, unsheathed blade at the ready, listening hard for the source of the delay. To the right, her best friend and grounder, Danny O'Leary, motioned toward a flickering candle in the window closest to the forest's edge. His pale green eyes were just visible over the top of the gray mask that covered his nose and mouth, and Keira saw them tighten in a silent question. Keira shrugged and shook her head slightly—she couldn't imagine why anyone would be awake inside.

The flame vanished as quickly as it had appeared, and after a moment's hesitation, the lead Legionnaire rose to his feet, motioning them forward once again. They continued their slow progress up the hill, one by one, stepping carefully to avoid the loudest patches of underbrush. Keira watched as the other black-clad figures slipped off in pairs, each going to their assault points. A light brush on her arm brought her attention back to Danny, who nodded toward the cellar door at the rear of the lodge. Reminded of their assignment, Keira took a deep breath, steeling herself for the task ahead.

Come on, Altman, don't screw this up.

The ramshackle lodge was intended to look deserted—a hiding place in plain sight—but a sharp eye could detect the signs of recent activity. Noticing that the grass by the cellar door was well-trampled, Keira glanced about nervously, scanning for guards who might come to investigate their activities. Danny tried the door handle gingerly, then more forcefully. As they'd guessed, it was latched from the other side.

Time for Plan B. Danny shifted away from the door, allowing Keira to kneel beside the handle while he readied himself to guard her back. It wouldn't do to have someone sneak up on her once she began the binding process.

Reaching deep inside herself, Keira gently nudged the mass of energy that lay just behind her stomach. Sending it downward through her feet, she firmly anchored herself to the grassy patch she'd chosen. Then, reaching out for the latch, she let the energy flow through her fingers as her lips puckered in a whistle. Called pneuma, or "breath," she knew the energy was too high for normal ears to detect. She felt this energy being twisted and shaped to match the waves of sound, and she altered the pitch of her note, letting it guide the pneuma into the shape she needed—wrought iron. All materials, and even people, had a shape to their pneuma, an amplitude and frequency to the energy holding them together. While a person's pneuma could change over time, the pneuma of objects like this lock remained a constant, unalterable touchstone.

She willed her pneuma to first match the iron's, then alter slightly, slowly disrupting its tidy molecular structure. The latch felt cold in her hand as it pulled the heat from her body, disordering the molecules that comprised it until the metal was nothing more than a molten blob. Grasping the ledge of the door, Keira eased it upward and heard the wood give way from its metal bindings with a dull *thunk*, revealing a set of earthen steps that led down into the cellar.

Danny began descending the stairs, longsword at the ready. They'd decided he'd go in first, to stall for time should they encounter anyone, and to give her the space to orchestrate a binding if needed. Following close behind, Keira nearly ran smack into Danny, who had frozen at the bottom of the steps. She halted, listening for the sound that had caught his attention. Bringing a finger to his lips, Danny inched forward again, deeper into the dank caverns of the cellar. Keira gripped the hilt of her sword and balled her left hand into a fist to hide its shaking.

You can do this. Just keep moving forward.

They were almost to the far end of the cellar now, and Keira could just make out the outline of the promised ladder leading to the main floor above. She barely registered the creak of a door hinge before something slammed her against the wall, sending her sword flying as the weight of a massive body pinned her to the ground.

Without thinking, Keira groped for its hairy neck, feeling the fiery breath as its jaws snapped inches from her face. Fear coiled in her belly, her limbs flailing in panic, her hands fumbling for the dagger she always carried at her hip.

Come on, come on!

The dog was squirming now, trying to wrestle out of her grip. She winced as its claws dug painfully into her thighs.

There!

Clutching her dagger by the hilt, she plunged it deep into the creature's side. Once, twice, three times—Keira kept stabbing, breathing heavily, ignoring its howls until she felt the giant body convulse and finally slump on top of her.

With a massive heave, she pushed its weight aside and rolled away from it. She heard Danny cursing nearby, and the clang of metal as he fought off his own seemingly more human assailant. She searched the floor desperately for her dropped sword, trying to ignore the potent scent of blood. Finally, her hands clasped smooth metal, and she scrambled to her feet, sword at the ready.

At the other end of the room, she saw the opened trapdoor spilling light into the dank cellar. Danny had reached the ladder before her. Keira hastened to follow him, emerging into a filthy larder to see him locked hilt to hilt with one of the conniving Marek Larghaen's hired men. Keira swore under her breath. They'd hoped to catch him unawares, but it seemed the old bastard had been warned, and had upped his guard to prepare for their arrival.

Keira sprinted toward her grounder, calling his name. Danny looked up and, with a great *umph,* spun the man he'd been grappling with in her direction just as she reached them. She met his back with her blade and felt an unsettling *crunch* as it slid through him. The man slumped against her, and she briefly bore his weight before letting him slide to the ground. He gurgled blood as Keira pulled her sword from his back, then was still.

"You okay?" Danny asked in his soft Boston-Irish lilt, quickly scanning her up and down.

Keira nodded. She couldn't seem to look away from the man at her feet. He was definitely dead—his eyes had that blank, dilated look that corpses get, and she could smell the piss and shit from his bowels, his muscles relaxed in death. Her mentor, Elliott, had told her the end wasn't pretty, but until this moment, she hadn't fully grasped the horror that would be her first kill. She swallowed hard, avoiding Danny's eyes. She wasn't ready for the understanding and sympathy she knew she'd find there.

Blinking furiously, Keira forced her gaze away from the body. "Fine," she muttered. "You?"

"I'll live."

She knew he wanted to say more, knew the moment when he thought better of it. She was grateful for that—Danny always seemed to know exactly what she needed.

"We should keep moving," Danny said. "On account of it seems like the others have run into trouble too. We need to get to Marek before he manages to pull off another of his grand escapes."

Keira nodded, noticing for the first time the sounds of fighting echoing from elsewhere in the lodge. She wadded up her confusing mix of emotions and flung them to the back of her mind. She'd have time to deal with them later. Peering around for an exit, Keira noted that the larder had seen better days. A thick layer of dust and grease covered the chopping tables and cabinetry, but the still-smoldering embers in the grand fireplace betrayed the room's recent use.

Shouts and curses echoed from the front rooms, but Keira and Danny instead headed for the servants' staircase in the back of the larder. The steps creaked as they swiftly climbed, making for the bedchambers on the floor above. They paused when they reached the landing, and Keira motioned toward a room on their left, where candlelight flickered beneath the closed door. Someone was definitely inside.

They flanked the door, one on either side, and Danny raised his eyebrows at her expectantly. She closed her eyes and concentrated on the pneuma. Slowly, Keira cast it out on the back of an inaudible whistle, searching with her mind for the presence they sought. The pneuma she encountered was twisted, dark, and calculating, but tinged with something else—a nervous tension of sorts. It was definitely Marek, all right, but he wasn't alone.

She could feel him pacing on the other side of the door along with two others, most likely bodyguards. Coming back to herself, she caught Danny's eye and held up three fingers. His brow furrowed. They'd been told Marek had only one bodyguard he trusted to share a room with him as he slept, and the original plan had been for her to muscle bind Marek while Danny took care of the bodyguard. Two guards threw that notion out the window, as she could only cast one bind at a time, and the out-of-body requirements of casting made her useless in a physical fight. That's why Danny was there—to guard her back during the process, and to help bring her back if she lost control. This would be difficult for him to do while fighting off two assailants at once.

She shook her head, and he nodded in response. Though the mask covered half his face, she knew he was grimacing underneath. They'd have to do this the old-fashioned way.

Danny grasped the door's handle while Keira mimed the general location of each of the three targets. Her fingers counted them down. *Three*...her grip tightened on the hilt of her sword... *two*...Danny's calm, determined eyes met hers...*one!*

With a shove, Danny flung open the door and rushed the closest bodyguard. Quick on his heels, Keira sprinted into the room and slammed into the other, meeting his sword with the clang of her own. She cursed her rotten luck—of course they had their weapons at the ready. No doubt they could hear the shouts echoing from the rest of the house.

She didn't have time to think about this long before she felt her sword drawn up and around in a giant arc, disentangling their blades and putting her immediately on the defensive. She barely blocked a crushing overhead swing. *This must be Rhondor*, she thought. *Marek's favorite.* Panic welled within her. *He's too big.*

She quickly squashed the panicked thought and forced herself to think rationally. *This is what you've trained for.* The man was enormous, and the broadsword he wielded nearly doubled his arm's reach. She needed to get some distance, or he'd skewer her for sure. After parrying his next slash, Keira managed to snatch up a ceramic plate from the table behind her. When Rhondor advanced again, she blocked his stroke while simultaneously shattering the plate against his head. He stumbled backward, allowing her a few precious seconds to regain her bearings.

From the corner of her eye, she saw a huddled figure creep along the edge of the room, making for the open hall door.

Oh no, you don't, she thought.

Shifting her sword into her left hand, using the other to snatch up her hip dagger and sent it flying end over end into Marek's side. The man cried out and doubled over in pain.

Keira grinned in satisfaction. *That'll keep him from getting too far.*

Before she could revel in her minor victory, Rhondor was on her again, and he was angrier than ever. Keira, remembering everything her mentor Nazor had ever taught her, spun out of his way, letting his momentum carry him into the wall behind. As she turned, she brought her blade down in a sweeping arc, slicing the giant man collar to navel. It wasn't a deep cut—certainly not mortal—but it was enough to slow his movements as he forced her back on the defensive, hammering her with slashes and stabs. He was tiring, but so was Keira. Her breathing was shallow, and her sword felt heavier with every block.

Rhondor's wound was bleeding freely now, forming a small pool at his feet. Sensing an opportunity, Keira retreated slightly. Rhondor immediately pressed his advantage and leaped toward her, his foot slipping on his own blood. He didn't fall, but he definitely stumbled.

That was all Keira needed.

She lunged forward, cutting a single stroke in and up, wedging her blade between the giant's ribs. He exhaled sharply as her sword pierced his diaphragm, then dropped to his knees, blood bubbling past his lips. She let him sag to the floor, then wrenched her blade free and spun to look for Danny.

He was in the opposite corner of the room, dealing the final blow to the other guard, a savage slice to the man's neck that left him in a gurgling heap. Danny turned toward her, and she saw a cruel cut down the side of his left arm. She started forward, brows knit with concern, but he waved her off.

"Just a scratch," Danny reassured her.

She nodded, not entirely convinced, but knew better than to argue just then.

"Where's Marek?" Danny asked.

Keira glanced around and cursed. "Damn it! He can't have gone far, not with my knife sticking out of his gut."

She saw a ghost of a smile cross Danny's face as he ran for the door. Out in the hallway, he bent to look at something on the floor before motioning her closer.

"Definitely blood. Seems you're not quite as hopeless at knife-throwing as Nazor says," he teased.

Keira scowled. "I told you I hit him. Honestly, I'm surprised he made it this far. From what they told us, I didn't take him for much of a fighter. His type always seems to have others around for the dirty work."

Danny's smile twisted darkly. "Never underestimate the survival instincts of a man like Marek. He didn't get to where he's at for lack of determination."

Keira nodded, gritting her teeth. She'd never met Marek Larghaen, but she knew enough about the snake to suspect that Danny was probably right. The slimy merchant had clambered over the backs of his fellow uplanders to become the local Tiarna's chief tax collector, keeping his power through threats, intimidation, and outright violence. *Yes*, Keira thought grimly, *he was certainly motivated, but that makes two of us.*

A clatter of metal hitting the floor brought their attention to a room at the far end of the hall. The two of them stealthily crept down the hall toward the sound, careful to check each room they passed to ensure they wouldn't be ambushed. As they approached the far door, Keira heard voices coming from inside—laughing, it sounded like. Danny pressed his ear to the door, a puzzled look on his face, then sighed in relief.

Throwing open the door, he and Keira entered to find a cowering Marek, surrounded by four of their fellow Legionnaires. Though masks obscured their faces, Keira quickly recognized their mentors, Elliott and Nazor.

"Nice of you both to join us," Nazor growled.

CHAOS LOOMING

CHAPTER TWO

"We were wondering where you'd gotten to," Nazor drawled, looking amused. Keira flushed, her face turning the deep shade of crimson for which it was famous.

"Well, you can thank us for slowing him down, at least. That's my knife sticking out of his hip," Keira shot back—too quickly, she now realized. Nazor's mouth twitched, and Keira's blush only deepened.

"You mean this?" Marek whimpered as Nazor's long fingers caressed the handle of Keira's blade. "Yes, we were just discussing it. Seems our friend here would very much like us *not* to touch it."

Marek nodded vigorously. "P-please. Just tell me what you want. Is it money? Jewels?"

His eagerness made Keira feel slimy. Of course he supposed they were a band of thieves, after his hard-earned—or, rather, *stolen*—cash. Nazor must have had a similar idea, as her black eyes suddenly narrowed. In one swift motion, she yanked the dagger from Marek's side.

The man howled, and the two hooded figures standing by Elliott and Nazor laughed savagely. Keira felt a bit sick as she stared at the blood flowing freely from Marek's side. She began to step forward, out of reflex, when she felt a firm hand grasp her wrist. Startled, she looked up to meet Danny's hardened face, his mouth set into a tight, immovable line. A small, almost imperceptible shake of his head reminded her that it wasn't the time to offer a bandage.

Nazor's face was an inch from Marek's now, the point of Keira's blade pressed firmly into the scum's left jugular.

"You think I want your blood money?" Nazor's words were barely a whisper, and Keira felt an icy shiver course down her spine. "You think I don't know how you got it? The lowlife rats you scrounged up to feed on the common river folk, on your own people?"

Beads of sweat trickled down Marek's cheek, mixing with the droplet of blood that had materialized on his neck.

"N-no, please. I'm only a merchant, an honest, hardworking merchant."

The other Legionnaires guffawed—even Elliott chuckled quietly, to Keira's surprise. She'd almost forgotten he was there. Elliott eyed Marek, a doubtful look in his eyes, but Marek didn't notice, too busy backtracking to care.

"I mean, maybe I have to grease a few wheels to get things done, but who doesn't? You wouldn't blame a roan for that, would ya?" He'd clearly seen the venomous look on Nazor's face and was trying desperately to right a swiftly sinking ship. "Who am I to turn down honest business over some misplaced scruples, I—aaah!"

Nazor had seized him by the collar and hauled him bodily to his feet. "I don't give a damn about your scruples," she snarled. "The only thing I care about is the four people killed this month by highway bandits—bandits paid for out of *your* coffers."

"Bandits? Surely not! I employ lawmen for—"

"*Lawmen?* Is that what you call brutes and thugs who take what they want and brutalize anyone who gets in their way?"

"I-I really can't imagine—"

"You're either a bastard or a fool, and I daresay it isn't the latter," Nazor said coldly. "Now, tell me, who else has benefited from your idea of 'scruples'?"

Marek blustered, and Nazor's grip on his shirt front tightened.

"Come on, slime, tell us who put you up to it."

The cowardly swine swallowed hard. "I-I can't. They'll see me dead."

"*We'll* see you dead if you don't tell us what we need to know."

Marek was sweating profusely by this point, his eyes darting from side to side like the cornered rat he was. He was almost pitiable—almost.

Nazor spat to the side in disgust. "Very well," she hissed, turning to Elliott. "Shall we bind him, then?"

Elliott shifted his weight from side to side, reaching up from crossed arms to rub the bridge of his nose, an old habit from his days of spectacle use. He gave Nazor an intent, searching look, and she matched it, unyielding in her question. They stood that way for a moment, their silence masking the intense flurry of activity going on behind those measured gazes.

Finally, Elliott sighed. "Indeed." He stepped toward Marek, leveling him with that same piercing gaze.

Before Keira could think, she felt her legs moving, heard her voice calling out.

"Wait!"

Six pairs of eyes turned to stare at her.

"Let me do it. I've been practicing spirit binds, and I could use the experience. It's part of the trial, right? During the rites?" Nazor wore a doubtful expression, but Keira pressed on, undeterred. "Danny can ground me—we've done it before."

Danny's wary eye told her he knew as well as she did that *before* meant on animals and willing participants only. She ignored him.

This is my chance, she realized, trying to get her breath under control, so as not to shatter the illusion of confidence. She watched as the others weighed her request. *This is my chance to prove myself.*

As a Legionnaire-in-training, she knew there was precious little opportunity.

It was Elliott who spoke.

"Very well, Keira. Prepare to perform the binding." Turning to Nazor, he explained, "If she's to perform the rites this summer, and become a full Legionnaire, she'll need the experience."

Nazor's face still showed her obvious skepticism, but she nodded, following Elliott's lead. Her grip loosened on Marek's collar, and she allowed him to collapse back onto his stool. She held fast to the dagger, though, and the look she gave him spoke all too clearly of her willingness to use it if provoked. Keira stepped toward Marek and assumed a wide-legged stance, rooting herself firmly in place.

"Slow your breathing, control it. In, then out." Elliott's voice was barely audible, but she calmed at once, feeling his support. She took a big breath in through her nose, out through her mouth, rooting herself into the floor. Then, closing her eyes, she reached for the ball of pneuma at her core. It responded almost instantly, unraveling until it flowed freely from her fingers. On an inaudible whistle, she cast it in Marek's direction. The pneuma coiled around him, smoothing out until it matched the pitch and kilter of his own spirit—the spirit of Marek.

The feeling of leaving her body didn't happen suddenly. It came on slowly, almost imperceptibly, until Keira realized with a start that she was becoming less *her* and more *them*.

She tasted his fear first and was struck by its metallic taste. He was afraid of the masked figures around him, but even more so, of—

The connection between them bucked and roiled as a wave of nausea threatened to overwhelm Keira.

He's fighting the binding, she realized almost absently, struggling to remain upright. A warm, firm hand grasped hers, and she felt herself flooded with familiar pneuma. *Danny.*

The nausea receded almost immediately. With Danny's pneuma tethering her in place, she was able to stretch out of herself, to wind around Marek more fully, settling into the exact shape and feel of his essence. Then the memories came, brutal and overwhelming.

A child held in the warm embrace of its mother.

Cold isolation as that same mother was lowered into a grave.

Harsh words and the violent slap of a drunken father.

Taking over the family business from that same abusive father.

Rising through the ranks of the merchant class, hiding his humble origins.

Being appointed a tax collector and finally getting the share he deserved.

Fear of the rumblings of a downtrodden peasant class.

Conviction that nothing and no one will take what is his.

The letter, threatening and veiled, yet oh so clear.

Leaving to purchase a larger ho—

The letter! Keira tried to stop the rushing tide of memories, tried to go back and get a better look. *What did the letter say? Who was it from?*

Marek's psyche rippled, as if realizing belatedly that it had an unwelcome intruder in its recesses. Keira was swimming upriver now, wading through memory and emotion, searching frantically for another glimpse of that letter. Marek fought her outright, trying to throw her off as the waves of his psyche tossed her about, ever more tumultuous in their fury.

Keira felt herself slipping and grasped desperately for some handhold in that sea of angry thoughts. Danny's hand tightened reflexively around hers, sensing her panic and seeking to draw her back. She fought him off, desperate to see what Marek was trying so hard to hide.

A muffled howl pierced her focus once more, and she realized they were up, standing, ready to make a run for it, knife in hand.

How did we get a knife? she thought distantly, still trying to hang on to Marek's mind. The gray-clad figures encircled them, and Keira felt Marek's growing panic, realized he'd risk it all in search of escape.

"Keira, come back!" someone yelled, fear filling his voice.

"Keira, you've lost control! He's throwing you off! Unbind, so we can stop him! Do it now!"

Keira struggled to do just that, but she was bound too tightly with Marek.

"I'm stuck," she whispered weakly.

Danny threw his pneuma toward her again, and she latched on, binding herself to him as tightly as possible, letting him pull her back. She felt herself slowly untangling from Marek's mind, and all at once, she was in her own body once more.

"I-I'm back," she panted.

It was precisely at this moment that she saw, through hazy vision, Marek lunge for the door, slashing savagely at the figure who stood in his way—at *Elliott*. Nazor appeared out of nowhere, stepping between them, her claymore spiraling in an elegant arc, cutting Marek down as deftly as she'd skim cream from milk.

That was it—he was gone. All of their hard work, for nothing. Keira's nose burned and her eyes watered, not only for the loss of the information they'd counted on so dearly to help the locals. She was genuinely sorry for the loss of *him*—Marek. That no-good, slime-ridden snake had made her weep for him, or rather, for the boy she'd seen in his memories. Bindings were notoriously intimate affairs, and she now knew him, *really* knew him, his hopes and dreams. She'd just seen them come to a bloody end, no sooner than she'd realized them, and that was damn near worth crying over, curse him.

Somewhere in all of this, Keira had collapsed to the floor, a fact she didn't realize until she felt Danny's sturdy arms lifting her gently to her feet. She was still wobbly, and so leaned heavily on him as they approached the others.

"I'm sorry," she muttered. "I thought I had it, but he got away from me." She cast pleading eyes toward Elliott, searching his face for understanding, for forgiveness. She found it in his kind eyes and breathed out a sigh of relief. She avoided Nazor's gaze, suspecting and not looking forward to what she'd find there.

"It's all right," Elliott assured her. "Bindings are no simple matters. What did you find out?"

Keira shifted through the jumble of memories she'd uncovered. "He received a letter a few months ago. There was something threatening about it, and I'm sure it has something to do with why he hired the bandits to loot the local trade routes."

"But who sent it?" Nazor's voice was icy. Keira glanced into her dark eyes, then quickly looked away, not wanting to deal with her disapproval quite yet.

"I-I'm not sure," she stammered. "The letter was marked with a purple seal, but I couldn't get a good enough look at it."

"Well, that's just excellent," Nazor snapped. "We've narrowed it down to everyone who's purchased purple wax over the last few years."

The burning sensation returned to Keira's nose. *Don't you cry, goddamn it*, she ordered herself. *Not now.*

Danny's grip on her tightened. "Keira did her best," he said defensively. "He was a slippery one—even I could feel that."

Keira thanked him silently, even as she figured Nazor would find this excuse irrelevant. Predictably, she snorted. Their training master turned away, barking a command at the other two Legionnaires.

"Come on, then, let's get *this*—" She nudged Marek's lifeless corpse with her toe. "—out of here."

Full of shame and just barely holding it together, Keira let Danny help her down the stairs, heading toward the rendezvous point before returning home.

~

THE NEXT MORNING, Keira was up and out of the house well before dawn, desperate to avoid both the pitying looks from Danny and frank disappointment from Nazor. She'd barely slept the night before, lying awake long after they'd returned to their farm, just outside the sleepy fishing village of Abalás. Looking back at the home she'd shared with Danny, Nazor, and Elliott these last few years, Keira was struck by the oft-avoided and yet familiar sensation that she didn't really belong here.

She made her way to the stable and was greeted warmly by her horse, Cerise, whose lips nibbled inquisitively at her ear as Keira began her daily grooming. Keira started at Cerise's flanks, methodically working on her chocolate brown withers with a round brush while trying hard not to dwell on the previous night's utter failure. She'd been so eager for this mission, ready to prove her worth to the Legion—and particularly to Nazor, who'd never hesitated to point out Keira's various deficiencies over the years.

So much for that, Keira thought ruefully.

She'd just started combing through Cerise's silken mane, carefully teasing apart the knots that seemed to magically accumulate mere hours after their last untangling, when Keira heard footsteps approaching. Stubbornly refusing to look up from her task, she attacked the knots with more vigor, determined that one thing in her life should be forced to cooperate as planned.

It was only when Cerise knickered in protest at her vigorous attentions that Keira looked up sheepishly to meet Elliott's gaze. One ruddy eyebrow was lifted in question.

"Be any rougher, and poor Cerise will require a wig fitting," he observed mildly in his clipped Oxford accent, "and I daresay that's not a good look on a horse."

Keira gnawed at her lip and slowed her frantic combing, rubbing Cerise's neck in apology. Never one to break a silence unnecessarily, Elliott selected a hoof pick and joined her labors in quiet camaraderie.

Grateful as ever for Elliott's comforting, non-confrontational demeanor, Keira continued her work in a more subdued fashion, still worrying at her lip. Eventually, though, Cerise and all the other horses had been groomed to perfection, the stalls mucked out, the tack room organized, and Keira realized with disappointed resignation that there was nothing left to distract her from the real task at hand. As always, Elliott seemed to sense her thoughts and had settled himself on a bench outside, the one they used for mending tack on fair weather days. His lanky legs stretched out before him as he leaned back against the fencepost to watch the rising sun. Keira joined him, sitting stiffly as she tried to find the right words. Finally, she settled for the obvious.

"I'm sorry."

Elliott didn't answer right away, and instead ran a hand through the shaggy, russet hair he preferred to leave untamed and falling past his ears on both sides. She'd begun to think he hadn't heard her when he suddenly spoke.

"I remember when you first arrived in Loren, Keira. So hurt and angry, confused about what it was we were even doing here. You're not alone, of course," he added, seeing Keira about to protest. "I've mentored dozens of Legionnaires over the centuries and through the various lives I've led. It's always the same—pulled so roughly from one world and dragged into another, it's only natural to be upset and disoriented. Pneumos may know the reason you were brought to this exact place and time, but we certainly don't."

Elliott shot Keira a crooked smile, and she met it briefly before kicking at some pine needles under her boot. He was right, of course. She'd spent five years in the small country of Loren, on this world they called Carnos, training to become a full Legionnaire, and she still found it difficult to grapple with the enormity of the Legion's calling. Hidden guardians who moved between worlds and whose tenure spanned multiple lifetimes, the Legionnaires' mere existence was a lot to take in.

"Do you remember the conversation we had about the nature of pneuma when you first arrived? You asked about the Legion, and I explained our mandate."

"Of course," Keira said. She'd heard that mandate repeated hundreds of times in the years since. "We create order from disorder, rebuild what has been destroyed, and heal what is broken."

Elliott nodded. "True, that is all true. But there is a qualifier. Do you remember it?" Seeing the quick shake of her head, he added, "We are to build *more* than we break and heal *more* than we destroy. It is a fundamental misattribution to believe that one can ever create order without *some* destruction. In fact," he continued, slipping smoothly into his nineteenth-century professor's voice, "as you know, everything in the universe trends toward greater and greater disorder. In your time, I'm told by other Legionnaires that the concept will be called 'entropy.' The universe is always expanding, leaving a void that must be filled, and the energy released by the creation of new worlds further fuels the universe's expansion. That is also how our pneumonancy works, of course. We harness the principles of entropy to disrupt the natural arrangement of atoms and molecules to create change in the world around us."

"My point," he emphasized, seeing Keira about to interrupt this endless monologue, "is that things naturally fall apart. Energy and matter delocalize, and order breaks down. The purpose of the Legion is, in many ways, to fight against entropy itself, to create order out of the chaos and prevent, or at the very least slow down, the gradual march of the universe toward inevitable chaos."

Keira rolled her eyes at the former Oxford professor, who was never one to forego a theoretical physics lecture tinged with philosophical implications. They'd had versions of this same debate before, but she decided to play along anyway.

"So, what you're saying is that it's a doomed purpose," Keira challenged, slipping easily into their usual back and forth. "The universe will continue to expand, disorder will increase because that's its nature, and all we can do is slow it down. Why even bother?"

Elliott cocked his head and grinned at Keira. "Who is to say what is truly natural? The world as it is now is not necessarily the world as it was meant to be. Besides, there is purpose to any fight, even if the end is known. Even when progress cannot be seen, that doesn't mean it's not there."

"But why *me*?" Keira asked, not for the first time. "Why am I here? Why did I have to be the one to die in a car crash and show up in an entirely new world?"

Elliott shook his head sadly. "I don't know, Keira. I can't tell you what the hinge point was that brought you and Danny here, or what it is you're meant to do. All I can say is that there is a reason, a *meaning* behind everything you've gone through, and everything you will go through. Of that I am certain."

Keira considered this, then remembered Marek's desperate struggle for control over his own mind, the way he'd fought against her—and won.

"It doesn't matter," she said miserably. "I *failed*, Elliott. I failed in the first important job the Legion trusted me with." She looked up at him, searching his face for some understanding. "All the practice and training—*years*, Elliott—and then I fail in front of everyone. How can they ever trust me as a Legionnaire now?"

Elliott eyed her, and she knew he was choosing his next words carefully.

"You didn't fail, Keira. You merely didn't succeed."

Keira snorted, which Elliott pointedly ignored. "Binding is about ordering the world around us, and I would remind you that we cannot hope to master the chaos of the world until we first confront the chaos within."

Keira laughed openly at that. "You sound like a fortune cookie."

"A what?"

Grinning, Keira shook her head. "Never mind."

Elliott gave her a considering look before asking, "Why didn't you have Danny ground you from the outset?"

The question caught her off guard, and Keira flushed with embarrassment. "I—well, I didn't think I'd need it." She tried to shrug off his probing stare, but continued to shift in her seat, gaze averted.

"What I mean is, what keeps you from reaching out to him when you need help?" Elliott pressed, though not unkindly. "You know the dangers of ungrounded pneumonancy. Push too far, and you'll become *undone*, your pneuma dissociated and your mind unable to return to your body. Why is it you wait for Danny to sense you're in danger before allowing him to intervene?"

Keira shivered at his words. Every Legionnaire had heard stories of the undone. Their bodies remained alive, but they were empty shells, utterly devoid of the people they'd once been. It was said that the Legion's council of elders could sometimes rejoin pneuma and body, but there was certainly no guarantee. Elliott was right—she did know the dangers.

She refused to meet his eye, refused to face the real question he was asking. When she didn't reply, Elliott cocked his head slightly, eyeing her intently. "Keira, I can't help but think there's something about the grounding process that you're avoiding," he said gently. "You and Danny arrived in Loren within a year of each other. The two of you are bound together as grounder and cantor, with a shared purpose here in Loren. There is no escaping it. I hope you know that."

Keira felt her face blush scarlet. She didn't like the direction this conversation was headed, and certainly didn't want to be discussing it with Elliott.

"You're right, of course," she said, keeping her tone light, almost flippant. "I was too cocky. I need to work on my control of the bind, avoid being so drawn into it. I'll do better next time, Elliot. I promise."

She could see the disappointment on his face, the knowledge that she was avoiding his actual question. Keira waited for him to press the issue, but slowly released the breath she'd been holding when he remained silent. She didn't want to think about why she had such difficulty letting Danny ground her, why she resisted that level of intimacy. To be so exposed and vulnerable, your every hope and fear on display to another person, was something she just couldn't bring herself to do. Understanding why would require a level of psychotherapy that she suspected was not readily available in Loren.

The two of them sat quietly for a moment, listening to the chatter of birds in the trees. "You've come a long way since you arrived," Elliott said finally, his warm smile extending to his twinkling amber eyes. "I'm proud of you."

Keira felt her throat tighten, her eyes suddenly stinging. *How was it*, she thought, *that he always knew the right thing to say?* It was largely thanks to Elliott that she'd found a home here, unexpected though the journey had been.

She watched as he languidly stretched and climbed to his feet, waving at her as he sauntered back toward the house. Elliott might be proud of her, but it wouldn't mean much if she couldn't prove herself to the Legion as a whole. They didn't keep dead weight on the payroll, as Nazor had frequently reminded her. Keira shivered at the thought of being left behind, alone and adrift in a foreign world, without friend or purpose.

She knew she'd ruined their chances of finding out who was truly behind the recent thefts and violence in Abalás. And if fighting chaos was the Legion's mission, she'd have to show them that she could contribute.

Tomorrow, she decided. *Tomorrow, I'll put everything right.*

ABOUT THE AUTHOR

H.B. Reneau is an author of fantasy and contemporary fiction. Author, physician, and proud dog mom, she is known for her character-driven, genre-crossing fiction that draws on her experiences in both medicine and the military. She has a particular love for strong female characters who face up to adversity and manage to subvert some expectations along the way.

To learn more, head over to her website at www.hbre neau.com. There you'll find her books, blog, and fun extras. Or reach out directly! Follow on social media and sign up for the monthly newsletter to receive receive free gifts, awesome discounts, and updates on all her latest projects.

If you enjoyed this book, please consider leaving a review at your favorite online storefront!

ALSO BY H.B. RENEAU

<u>The Legion of Pneumos</u>

Chaos Looming

Haven Enduring

<u>The Legion of Pneumos: Novella Collection</u>

The Cantor

The Centus

The Rebel

The Remnant